9781784979300

# THE CASE OF
THE SEVEN WHISTLERS

# BY
# GEORGE BELLAIRS

DEATH OF A BUSYBODY
MURDER WILL SPEAK
DEATH STOPS THE FROLIC
THE MURDER OF A QUACK
CALAMITY AT HARWOOD
DEATH IN THE NIGHT WATCHES

*This is a work of fiction, the characters are entirely imaginary, and no reference to any person living or dead is implied.*

# THE CASE OF
# The Seven Whistlers

### GEORGE BELLAIRS

*"When seven such birds are seen together, they are called the seven whistlers, and their musical chorus bodes ill or harm to those who hear it."*

CHARLES HARDWICK

*NEW YORK*
THE MACMILLAN COMPANY
*1948*

Copyright, 1948, By
George Bellairs.

ALL RIGHTS RESERVED—NO PART OF THIS BOOK MAY BE REPRODUCED IN ANY FORM WITHOUT PERMISSION IN WRITING FROM THE PUBLISHER, EXCEPT BY A REVIEWER WHO WISHES TO QUOTE BRIEF PASSAGES IN CONNECTION WITH A REVIEW WRITTEN FOR INCLUSION IN MAGAZINE OR NEWSPAPER.

First Printing

PRINTED IN THE UNITED STATES OF AMERICA

## CONTENTS

1. THE SEVEN WHISTLERS — 1
2. WHEEL IN THE BODY — 7
3. SQUABBLE AT THE SARACEN'S HEAD — 17
4. THE MISSING KEY — 28
5. MOTIVE? — 38
6. THE RIVALS — 49
7. MARK CURWEN'S BOX — 59
8. RIDGFIELD'S HOTEL — 67
9. THE SECOND KEY — 76
10. THE SEVEN WHISTLERS AGAIN — 87
11. ALIBI AT THE PALACE — 99
12. MONEY IN THE BANK — 110
13. THE APPEARANCE OF BIRDIE JAMESON — 119
14. CIGARETTE ENDS — 129
15. DEATH ON BLIGHT HEAD — 136
16. THE ROOM ABOVE THE SHOP — 147
17. THE "MAID OF MORVEN" — 157
18. THE TOWING PATH — 166
19. A FRESH START — 178
20. THE QUIET HOUSE — 187

## 1

### THE SEVEN WHISTLERS

ON the last day of her holiday at Fetling-on-Sea, Miss Selina Adlestrop rose early to buy antiques. On the previous evening, after it had closed, she had seen in the bow window of a curiosity shop the very oak chest she had been hunting for years. She had hardly slept a wink all night lest someone should buy it before her. She was on the doorstep at opening time on the morrow.

The shop itself stood in a narrow street which climbed uphill from the fishing quay to the modern part of the town. There were about sixty steps in the street which gently mounted the incline. Seven steps, then a cobbled slope; then seven more steps . . . And so on, to the top. Tall houses with walled gardens flanked it, and the trees from the gardens hung over it and interlaced their leaves in the summer. Very pleasant. Miss Adlestrop was very fond of the street. It reminded her of Paris. She had once spent a week in Paris on a conducted tour, since when, as with most sentimentalists, the place had been mixed up in a lot of fantastic dreams. She, dear romantic spinster, was not alone in such visions. Hard-headed business men have been known to dissolve into hogwash in similar circumstances. One of them wanted to buy the street entirely and build an arcade of olde Englyshe shoppes in it. Fortunately it belonged to the Corporation of the town, who knew better than to part with it . . .

Half way up the slope stood the antique shop of Messrs. Grossman and Small. Over the door swung a painted sign bearing the picture of seven birds arranged in a triangle, and the superscription, "THE SIGN OF THE SEVEN WHISTLERS," *Grossman and Small, Prop'rs*. The birds themselves were plovers, although you wouldn't have thought it to look at them. The man who first hung the sign had a sense of humour. He was a Jew, named Feinmann. You could make out his name dimly beneath those of the present proprietors, who had had it painted out when they took over. The Whistlers is the legendary name for the Wandering Jews and Mr. Feinmann chuckled as he selected it for his trade sign. He only got half a tale, however. The rest is that they are birds of ill-omen. Perhaps had poor Mr. Feinmann known that he wouldn't have enjoyed the joke so much. He used to sit among his Sheraton chairs and Welsh dressers reading the Song of Songs, for he loved a young Jewess with eyes like a timid deer. And when she ran away with the man from the souvenir shop higher up, Mr. Feinmann drank salts of lemon. That is how his name came to be painted out . . .

As we were saying, Miss Adlestrop stood under the painted sign before the shop door was unlocked. Inside, Messrs. Grossman and Small could be seen circulating among the old furniture and lovely china, glass and pottery in which they specialised. The windows and door were glazed in old green bottle-glass and behind it the partners looked like a large and a small fish floating in a clear sea.

Miss Adlestrop had had dealings with *The Seven Whistlers* in the past. The proprietors' names seemed somehow to have got mixed up, however, like the displaced tags on the relics of a bargain sale.

Mr. Grossman was a tiny man of about five feet two, with small hands and feet and the slim figure and grace of movement of a ballet dancer. His thin sensitive face, clean and the colour of pale terra cotta, was topped by glistening white hair. His taste in glass, pottery and old lace was fastidious and impeccable. He left the bulk of the cumbersome furniture to his colleague, Small.

Small was an enormous man with a huge paunch which hung between his knees when he was sitting. He had solid limbs like the branches of an old tree and a round florid face. His head was shaped like an orange and topped by a brown, ill-fitting wig. His thick, sloppy lips, large Roman nose, small shifty eyes and ill-fitting clothes finished off an appearance more like that of a shady broker's man than an expert in old furniture and prints.

How this incongruous pair got together Miss Adlestrop couldn't even guess.

She much preferred Mr. Grossman. Mr. Small drank heavily, as his complexion and breath advertised. On the other hand, Mr. Grossman never touched a drop. He had confessed as much to Miss Adlestrop once in the excitement of selling her some hollow-stemmed champagne glasses for far more than they were worth. His father had drunk himself to death, he whispered, and he was afraid he might do the same himself if he started. Miss Adlestrop's cousin Jonas had died that way. He had tried to throw some heliotrope snakes through the window of his bedroom and somehow got mixed up with them and hurled himself down three storeys as well as the snakes. This seemed a bond in common between Miss Adlestrop and Mr. Grossman.

She had an idea that in some way Mr. Grossman and Mr. Small were relatives, but she never discovered how. The link between them seemed to be their assistant, Mrs. Doakes, a tall, muscular, good-looking woman with bleached hair, painted nails, a slight cast in one eye when you gave her a straight look, and a way of exciting men whilst putting women out of countenance. This woman called both partners 'uncle' and behaved as if she owned the shop. Miss Adlestrop, who suspected that Mrs. Doakes was no better than she should be, always gave her a wide berth.

"The box?" said Mr. Grossman, prancing up to Miss Adlestrop, shaking her by the hand like a long lost friend and with the other adjusting a Dresden figure which had got too near the edge of the table on which it was standing. "The box? Thirty-five pounds, Miss Adlestrop. A bargain!"

He rubbed his palms together like an acrobat about to do an exacting trick, and rocked himself to and fro on his heels and toes.

Miss Adlestrop turned large astonished eyes on the dealer. She had a small button nose, like a whiteheart cherry, little heart-shaped lips and a timid, faltering manner which stood her in very good stead and hid her shrewdness in striking a bargain. She began to handle Toby jugs, Staffordshire salt-glaze figures, and an old punchbowl decorated with red and green sprays of apples and plums.

"It's an old and very interesting piece," persisted Mr. Grossman, who was up to all the tricks of cunning buyers. "Quite unique of its kind. It belonged to Mr. Mark Curwen who died a month or so ago. Ask any local collector about Mark Curwen's box. He'll tell you it's over three hundred years old . . ."

"Any worm-holes in it?" demanded Miss Adlestrop, who had already, in her own way, made quite sure there weren't.

Mr. Grossman raised his eyes to heaven and vehemently denied it.

The shop was filling up. Trippers with plenty of money and little in the normal way to spend it on were rummaging round for expensive souvenirs, silver tea services and what not, to take home and give or show their admiring friends. Two sailors were buying trinkets from Mrs. Doakes who was displaying her physical charms as well as rings and brooches.

One of the sailors was obviously impressed and looked ready to ask her if she was free after business hours . . .

"Twenty-five pounds!" suddenly said Miss Adlestrop.

Mr. Grossman again raised his well-kept hands in horror, and gracefully recoiled taking care to avoid a table crowded with old sherry glasses.

"I'm sorry; thirty is the least we can take. Even then we'd have to sacrifice all our profit on the deal . . ."

Battle was properly joined. It was like a boxing match. They argued, were silent, pondered and retired to consult their own minds. The bout was punctuated by Mr. Grossman's being called away several times by other customers. These pauses, like those granted by the ringside gong, gave the protagonists time to gather their energies for further efforts . . .

As Miss Adlestrop wrote a cheque for twenty-seven pounds ten shillings, Mrs. Doakes and Mr. Small smiled at their colleague behind her back . . .

Mark Curwen's box had been knocked down at the auction to Mr. Grossman for fifteen pounds. It had seen better days. But Grossman and Small, at the sign of *The Seven Whistlers,* knew all about that. They filled in the worm-holes with boot polish, replaced one of the legs which was suffering from dry rot, by a more solid one, and gave the whole a good wax-polishing.

Miss Adelstrop descended the steep street well satisfied. She thought she had won the contest, and almost fell headlong a time or two through absent-mindedly pondering where she should put her new box, and seeing visions of numerous admiring neighbours standing before it awestruck. . . .

Mr. Grossman had promised to see the chest safely on its way for delivery at Miss Adlestrop's home in Hartsbury. She hardly cared to trust it to the tender mercies of the railway. Or of a carrier for that matter. But she couldn't carry it home herself, so had to be content. *The Seven Whistlers* had promised to pack it securely and cover it for transport in plenty of good hessian covers.

Her head on one side and still a bit doubtful about leaving her prize to the tender mercies of a third party, Miss Adlestrop made her way back to the sedate private hotel she visited twice every year, and spent the rest of the morning packing . . .

At *The Seven Whistlers* Mr. Grossman and Mr. Small were quarrelling. They were always squabbling about something . . .

## 2

## WHEEL IN THE BODY

"RICHARD! Richard! Come 'ere and give an 'and...."
Sam Biles, porter, head cook and bottle-washer at Hartsbury Station, yelled across the line to his underling, a fat youth in a shabby blue suit which he had outgrown, engaged in carrying boxes of day-old chicks from the platform to the luggage-office.

Richard Cramp slowly deposited a chirping parcel on a bench, slowly climbed down on the line, slowly crossed it and slowly levered himself upwards to Sam's side.

"An' get a move on, young Dick."

To call Richard Cramp "Dick" was an insult. His mother said so, and what his mother said was right. Richard it was, after his mother's cousin with money in Australia, and Richard it had to be.

Young Cramp was undecided whether or not to give notice. He had been measured for a railway uniform and handed in the requisite number of clothing coupons, but his panoply still hadn't arrived after three months' waiting. He suspected that the stationmaster at Fetling had bought a new Sunday rig-out at his expense. And now "Dick"!

"*Richard,*" he said to his superior officer and glared.

"Don't be insulent," replied Sam, who regarded Richard's education very seriously, for he had attended the village school with his father and took it hard when the latter fell and drowned himself in a vat of stout at the local brewery. Judging from the amount of such stuff Cramp senior had disposed of in his lifetime, death came in a kindly congenial way . . .

"Don't be insulent. Give an 'and with this box. The things that Adlestrop woman buys and burdens us with . . . Addlepate she oughter be called. This thing met be made of iron or somethin'. It's as 'eavy as lead . . ."

Richard scratched his head at this mixed problem in specific gravity and took one end of the load.

"Oo! Cripes!!!"

The two strained and groaned and hoisted and got the large burden on a truck. It was Mark Curwen's box, sewn up in sacking and packing, and addressed to Miss Adlestrop, Brook Cottage, Hartsbury.

"Now, now, Richard. Langwidge! Langwidge! And you come along wi' me and help carry it in the 'ouse. An' no hanging round for tips. That's my privilege . . . me bein' senior man o' the two and I'll see you don't suffer for it . . ."

"Umph . . ."

"An' wot, might I ask, is the meanin' o' that noise you jest made?"

In the very middle of Miss Adlestrop's *At Home* for the Hartsbury Women's Guild, the railway company arrived with their precious cargo, Richard pulling and Sam pushing and balancing the box on the truck.

Inside the house a dozen or so women were knitting, sewing and gossiping, mostly the latter, whilst in the kitchen an elderly maid was preparing a light tea with the help of a hired village girl, who was very good looking in a rustic fashion and to whom Florence, the maid, was giving what she thought good advice on affairs of the heart. This wisdom was entirely negative, for Florence was a man-hater and regarded every member of the opposite sex as a deceiver and seducer.

She put a dose of margarine on a piece of bread and then set about scraping it off again.

"There's 'ardly a house in this village where you couldn't point to some hidden tragedy or other, entirely due to the deceitfulness of men . . ."

She jerked her head forward like a snake striking and glared at the girl as though she had already caught her in some misdemeanour.

"Yes, Miss Furlong," said Anne, giving her superior officer a wide-eyed look which embodied in eighteen and a half years more worldly wisdom than Florence had accumulated in fifty.

"And don't stand there gawkin'. Put that teapot to warm . . ."

Whereupon the railway truck appeared and caused differing reactions in the two feminine bosoms.

To Florence, Sam Biles, a widower, was the devil in disguise; an amorous beast who had once tasted matrimonial blood and was on the prowl for more. To Anne, young Richard would have been a bit of all right if he hadn't looked as though he'd once put on a suit that fitted him and then inflated himself until it retreated half way up his arms and legs and strained at every button.

In the living quarters of the cottage, the Dorcases ceased work, and fourteen of them gathered round the window to watch Sam and his assistant toil and moil with their burden. These two struggled, grumbled and only with difficulty straightened their knees under the load. They certainly couldn't straighten their backs.

Over the red tiles of the kitchen the bearers scuffled their way to the sitting-room.

Another figure appeared from the scullery at the back. A thin, scraggy, tough-looking woman who *did* for Miss Adlestrop daily. Whereas Florence and Anne were bare-headed, the char wore a shapeless black hat and worked in it. This was a form of below-stairs etiquette closely akin to the ecclesiastical rule which forbids a female in church bare-headed. A sort of graduate's cap worn to show that the daily help didn't live in and as such was independent to come and go as she liked, and wearing headgear as a reminder of the fact.

" 'Ellish 'eavy," ground out Sam, forgetting himself.

"Mister Biles!!!" gasped Miss Adlestrop suddenly materialising. "How dare you swear in my house?"

And she dismissed him without a tip to punish him.

"Come you 'ere at once't and get the paste in these sangwidges," shouted Florence to her aide-de-camp, for her eagle eye had spotted Anne exchanging amorous glances with the fat boy . . .

In the centre of the village, a hundred yards or so away, P.C. Donald Puddiphatt stood perspiring from every pore and puffing like a traction engine as he argued with Seth Hale, the local joiner and undertaker. They were an ill-assorted couple. One looked to have been poured into his uniform which fitted him skin-tight owing to his ever increasing size; the other was nearly as fleshless as a skeleton with old clothes hanging from his bony body like washing on a clothes horse.

They were talking politics. Behind them on the wall were two warring posters.

*VOTE FOR BLANKET*
*The Man You Can Trust*
*He's Served You Well*

Next Thursday See That It's
BLANKET, Wilbraham ....X
Galloper, Joe .............—

*VOTE FOR GALLOPER*
*The Labour Candidate*
*Let's Have a Change This Time*

Away with Complacency. So Next Thursday:
Blanket, W. ...............—
GALLOPER, Joe .........X

The bobby had thrust his helmet on the back of his head to cool his brow on which the sweat looked to be bubbling at boiling point. The joiner wore a battered billycock which his ears prevented from falling over his eyes.

"Now, my old father allus said as the Tories . . ." intoned P.C. Puddiphatt.

This was his modest way of expressing his own profound and original thoughts. His parent, who had peacefully lain in the churchyard for ten years or more, never got a word in edgeways during his wife's lifetime, for she never stopped talking even in her sleep, and he died immediately after her, some said from the shock of silence.

"Now my old father allus said . . ."

We shall never know what he said *à propos* Blanket and his kind, for a stream of yelling women poured out of Brook Cottage, surrounded the constable and bore him back and indoors by sheer weight of numbers.

And somehow, Seth Hale was included in the throng and carried along with the bobby, like a piece of waste paper set dancing and jigging and drawn in its path by an express train passing through a station.

As he entered the living room of the house, P.C. Puddiphatt gasped and his eyes slowly emerged from their sockets and looked like taking on a separate and astonished existence of their own apart from his body. The place was a bedlam. Women screaming, laughing, weeping. Three bodies, including that of Miss Adlestrop, lying on the floor, with Mrs. Hollis, the one with the hat, smacking faces, administering water, smelling salts and sal volatile.

"All about wun little body!" Mrs. Hollis kept muttering. She was the parochial layer-out of corpses and hence rather contemptuous of death in all its forms.

Puddiphatt, followed by the joiner, who looked more like a skeleton than ever, and performed a sort of *danse macabre* in the policeman's huge wake, gazed around in bewilderment. Was it a case of mass slaughter?

Mrs. Hollis soon put them right. Leaving her patients, she strode with great determination to the oak chest which stood amid a litter of sackcloth and unconscious women, and flung back the lid.

The constable gingerly approached and peered cautiously inside the box, as though expecting a swarm of troubles to fly out and smother him. He gasped and clawed at the chest for support . . .

Inside, with his knees bent and his head lolling on them like an exhausted child sleeping, was little Mr. Grossman!

The policeman bent and prodded the body with a fat forefinger.

"Why! He's cold and stiff," he mumbled as though making a phenomenal discovery. And not knowing quite how to behave next, he removed with difficulty his helmet and bowed his head reverently.

Two more women then fainted, another dissolved into hysterics and had her face smacked by Mrs. Hollis, and Mr. Hale, the joiner, fell unconscious to the ground with a great rattle of bones.

By this time, Miss Adlestrop had inhaled enough ammonia and burnt feathers to pull her back to consciousness, and pointing a limp hand in the direction of the garden, muttered, "Uncle Alfred . . . Mr. Councillor Blanket . . ."

Whereupon Mrs. Hollis walked to a bell-push prominently fixed on the wall and pressed it. The result was a hullaballo like that made by a fire-engine in full cry and an American police car out quietly to round up a gang of killers. This racket of bells and klaxons started outside a small shack like a hen-coop at the far end of the vegetable garden and brought forth two men, one like John Bull and the other like Ben Turpin.

John Bull was Councillor Blanket, shortly to have his popularity and worth tested at the Rural District Council elections. He was the village wiseacre. He knew, or professed to know, all about farming, flour-milling, quarrying and shopkeeping, which were the principal ways of earning a living in Hartsbury. He was always here, there and everywhere telling you what to do and how to do it. He was also a homœopathist, and if in his presence you complained of a cold, he would press upon you small pillules of *Camphor, Aconitum Napellus* and *Arsenicum Album*. More complicated complaints also tackled . . . He looked made-up for the part of John Bull, like an actor just ready for the footlights. Grease-painty complexion, tufts of hair, bald head with puffs of white at the side complete. . . .

His companion was a little rabbity man with a squint and a ragged moustache. Mr. Alfred was Miss Adlestrop's uncle and under her protection, for he was locally said to be ninepence to the shilling, if you understand the term. He was eccentric and an inventor. His inventions never earned him any money but were widely known in the locality. For example, the alarm system which brought him from the hut in which he lived to the rescue of the feminine section of the family in the house was a child of his brain. It was used when tramps, hawkers or strange men called and wouldn't be gainsaid. Uncle Alfred always promptly answered the loud call to duty and invariably caused great mirth and greater truculence from the offenders he had ostensibly arrived to chuck out. Other inventions to his credit were an alarm nest-box which rang a gong when a hen laid in it; an automatic shotgun which discharged itself every ten minutes to scare off crows from crops; a rabbit snare which sounded a siren when it caught anything; and a mole-trap which rang a bell in your bedroom when it functioned. There was a ring, a hoot or an explosion with every product of uncle's brain and his workshop, convertible into a small living-room, bedroom or bathroom on pulling a specified lever which rang a bell to show that it was operating, was always in eruption. The discovery of the body provided a welcome relief to Mr. Blanket, for Alfred was trying to persuade him to invest in thief-proof ballot-boxes for the election—a horn sounded if you tried to extract a voting-paper—in exchange for his cross opposite the councillor's name. . . .

The two men broke into a shambling trot down the garden and gradually accelerated, Uncle Alfred running so fast that you couldn't see his legs going, like a mouse, and John Bull lumping along steadily, his head held firmly erect to keep his hat from falling off.

By the time they arrived, P.C. Puddiphatt had the body on the floor. Not having handy his volume of *The Policeman's Vade Mecum*, which he consulted on all extraordinary occasions, and feeling that some action was expected of him by the crowd of helpless women, he had hoisted Mr. Grossman, deceased, from his resting place, laid him on the rug and was prodding him with two fingers as though trying to rouse him from sleep.

"Wonder whether artificial resp'ration 'ud be any use?" he was asking himself for the benefit of the ladies when the huge form of Mr. Councillor Blanket filled the doorway and then entered and almost filled the room.

A great calm fell upon the place as this mountainous know-all put in an appearance. His prominent eyes fell upon the village constable and the corpse he was auscultating.

"What do you think you're doing there, Puddiphatt?"

Whereupon the poor constable leapt to his feet and saluted, although he had no reason for doing so, and the unconscious women recovered through the stimulus of the booming voice.

"Jest wonderin' whether to artificial respirate, sir . . ."

"You . . . you . . . you. Can't you see that *rigor mortis* has already set in upon the cadaver?" explained the councillor, like an anatomist ready to dissect before a flock of students.

"Um . . . Ah . . ."

"You want to send for the police . . ."

"But I'm the police . . ."

"YOU!!"

Whereupon John Bull took up Miss Adlestrop's telephone without so much as a by-your-leave, and called for a doctor and the Sergeant of Police at Gosley-in-the-Marsh, the nearest headquarters.

"Leave everything as it is," he commanded, and in their anxiety to obey the oracle, many of the women stood to attention like pillars of salt.

Uncle Alfred closely inspected the box, apparently turning over in his mind the feasibility of installing some sort of alarm signal to function should another corpse be dumped in it.

"Leave that alone, Alfred," said Mr. Blanket irritably. And then he pulled from his pocket his portable medicine case of homœopathic remedies. "Some of you ladies look a bit seedy after this experience. Let's see what we can do. Florence, just get me a jug and some water and glasses. Now for shock . . . Let me see . . . *Veratrum Viride* . . . yes, yes . . . *Similia similibus curantur* . . . Like cures like . . ."

Like an alchemist muttering the potent words, Mr. Blanket mixed and dispensed his potions. . . .

P.C. Puddiphatt stood to attention on the hearthrug, wishing he'd got his *Vade Mecum* before he appeared on the scene. . . .

The homœopathist rounded up the women like a good sheep-dog and drove them into the next room. The bobby, the corpse and Uncle Alfred were left together keeping watch. . . .

## 3

### SQUABBLE AT THE SARACEN'S HEAD

LORD TROTWOODE, chairman of the local railway company, grew impatient of the county police investigation of *The Seven Whistlers* crime after the first day.

Already, two factions had arisen in the neighbourhood. One treated the delivery of a corpse neatly folded in an oak chest by the railway with apprehension. The company became the centre of alarmist agitation. People were terrified of travelling alone in compartments. Some declined to make a journey at all by train and joined 'bus queues. Others saw homicidal maniacs hiding in every waiting-room, warehouse and siding. The other section, which had suffered long from trains running hours behind schedule, uncomfortable carriages, and surly officials, saw in the tragedy a cheap source of ridicule. They laughed and passed round jokes about travellers dying of boredom and exhaustion during slow progress.

Lord Trotwoode's patience, of which he had not a large stock, gave out over lunch at *The Saracen's Head,* Fetling, two days after the crime, the solution of which still eluded the local police.

His Lordship, infuriated by finding in his boiled pudding a piece of the cloth in which it had been cooked, looked round for a victim in the absence of any of the waiters, who for long periods seemed to become invisible. At a nearby table the Chief Constable was blandly dining with the local Member of Parliament, as though murders and suffering railways didn't exist at all.

Lord Trotwoode disentangled the pudding cloth from his false-teeth, glared hard at the Chief Constable, turned a dirty red and rushed across to him.

Colonel Carslake looked up mildly from the peach melba he was obviously enjoying and smiled agreeably.

"Mornin', Trotwoode," he said.

The peach melba was the last straw. His Lordship had been told that there was no choice of sweets and had been served with jam roll and a piece of old rag. And here was Carslake with an ice. It was . . .

"Damme, man. Get on with findin' the murderer at large in this district and presumably plannin' another crime among our rollin' stock, instead of dallyin' over food—and damn rotten food at that—or I'll complain to the Home Secretary . . ."

Colonel Carslake slapped his spoon down in the remains of his water ice, which tasted of powdered milk, and rose to the challenge. All eyes were upon him. A pretty scene of wrangling and abuse began, too shocking and childish to chronicle here. It may be heard in detail from anybody who dined there that day. The food was forgotten. The brawl eclipsed all else, and the local M.P., fearing that any taking of sides on his part might cost him votes at the next general election, suddenly spotted a warm supporter in one corner and, offering excuses to his host, which weren't heard above the din of battle, he slid away to accept an invitation to a garden-party of which he had previously determined to fight shy. . . .

The upshot of it all was that the Chief Constable telephoned to Scotland Yard that afternoon. . . .

Detective-Inspector Littlejohn, of the Metropolitan C.I.D.,

arrived at county headquarters, Fetling-on-Sea, the following morning.

Superintendent Gillespie of the county force was in charge of the case. He was fed-up with it already, for he had been subjected to a series of pep-talks about it by the Chief Constable, who seemed to be under the impression that clues grew on trees and merely awaited the picking and that a case should be solved, like an African campaign, by concentrating a lot of men on it and doing a lot of planning beforehand.

Colonel Carslake, tall, thin, peppery and self-important, said he was glad to see Littlejohn, looked him up and down as though he were the new batman, gave him a pep-talk and then went off for a day's shooting.

Gillespie was very helpful. Littlejohn liked him at once, although he was puzzled as to how he had ever got in the Force. For Gillespie was slightly knock-kneed and bad on his feet. This was due to his jumping fully clothed into the canal on one occasion and bringing out a half-drowned child, which he saved by artificial respiration instead of changing his clothes, thereby giving himself a number of arthritic complaints. But, of course, he didn't tell Littlejohn that. He had also a reputation for eccentricity, due, it was conjectured, to the state of his liver. He would go for days without speaking to anyone and then suddenly change into bouts of great jocularity. . . .

It was one of Gillespie's off-periods when Littlejohn arrived. He hadn't spoken to any of his subordinates, except to order them about, for three days, but he had to stir himself a bit when his visitor appeared. He sat there, like a melancholy sea-lion propped up at a desk, and detailed a lot of painstaking work and a confused assortment of information. He had his hat on. He always wore it in the office when his liver was wrong side out. He said there was a draught from the windows, even when they were closed.

The deceased had lived in a flat in Fetling, alone, and attended by a daily woman who cleaned up for him and generally saw to his comfort. His partner, Small, had his quarters over the business premises at *The Seven Whistlers*.

"Queer name," said Littlejohn, interrupting.

Gillespie looked disgusted.

"As soon as anybody sets up a café, antique shop or curio place in a town like this, they think they have to give it a damn' silly name. The main tea-rooms here are called *Fred's Pantry*, and there's neither a pantry nor a Fred. And then there's another, *The Cherry Orchard*, right in the High Street, with no cherries or orchards for miles. And now this *Seven Whistlers* . . . What do they want to whistle for, and why seven, and why call the blasted place . . . ?"

He paused and looked a bit sheepish.

"Sorry, Inspector Littlejohn. This case is getting on my nerves. The Chief's been awful . . . Pestered us to death . . . What about a cup of tea?"

Littlejohn wasn't very fond of constabulary tea, but he agreed. It was served in thick cups and boiling, as usual, and whilst Littlejohn waited for his to cool, Gillespie took three pillules from a bottle labelled *Podophyllum* and washed them down with a mighty draught of the scalding liquid without turning a hair.

Yes, Small had his quarters over *The Seven Whistlers*. He was Grossman's brother-in-law. He had married his late partner's sister as second wife and she had been dead for years.

"Did the two of them get on well together?" asked Littlejohn.

"Oh, yes. I've been thoroughly into that. How they came to be associated, I can't for the life of me think. Grossman was a little, mincing, fastidious chap. Almost ladylike in his ways. And Small's a great hulking brute of a fellow, drinks heavily and looks like a bruiser. You can well imagine him and Grossman getting on one another's nerves and Small outing his partner, stuffing him in the oak chest and sending him on his travels. But it's not as easy as that. Small's got a good alibi. . . . Tell you about it when we get to that. . . ."

The police-station was an old building in a backwater facing the graveyard of the parish church, the clock-chimes of which punctuated the interview every quarter-hour. There was a funeral in progress and the mourners had to struggle to keep themselves upright against the stiff breeze blowing from the sea. The parson's vestments flapped at right-angles to his body. The bearers staggered beneath their burden and tottered from side to side as they advanced to the graveside. Tall, tortured trees surrounded the churchyard, leaning at an angle caused by the fury of the prevailing winds.

Gillespie sadly eyed the funeral procession and went on with his tale.

"There's another party in the shop, too. A Mrs. Doakes. She's Small's niece by his first marriage and keeps house for him. She's married to a sailor . . . Officer in the Merchant Navy. I don't care for her . . ."

"Why?"

"Oh, dunno, really. A bit uppish . . . and on the loose. That sort don't appeal to me."

Littlejohn was sure they didn't.

"Medical evidence shows that Grossman had been dead since about nine o'clock on the night before he was delivered at Miss . . . Miss . . . Adlestrop's—damn silly name—Miss Adlestrop's house in the box. Cause of death, suffocation. Seems he was rendered unconscious by a crack on the head and locked in the box to die . . ."

"Nasty . . ."

"Very nasty . . ."

The church clock chimed half-past twelve and Gillespie

started, drew a large watch from the side pocket of his trousers and consulted it.

"Good heavens! Twelve-thirty already. Lunch time. Come and have a bit of food and then we'll carry on after. The inquest's at two, so we can go there together if you like. You'll get a lot of information first-hand then . . . Medical and the like. Eh?"

"All right to me, sir."

"Good. One thing, though. We'll not discuss the case over lunch, if you don't mind. I'm bothered with my digestion and the doctor says I must relax over my food. So we'd better change the subject. Don't mind, do you?"

Littlejohn said he didn't mind at all. On the contrary . . . But he groaned within him, for he anticipated a very boring session. Gillespie looked like making very poor company.

They lunched at *The Saracen's Head*. They were undisturbed except for casual greetings from acquaintances of Gillespie, which he didn't return in many cases and in others very curtly on account of his liver. They all understood and expected that next week it would be all right and he would be slapping them on the back and roaring pleasantries at them.

Littlejohn was pleasantly surprised at the lunch, and even more pleased with Gillespie's company. The Superintendent turned out to be an enthusiastic pigeon-flyer in his off-hours and warmed to his subject and held Littlejohn spellbound. He even took the Scotland Yard man by the arm, led him to the window, showed him the old pigeons in the square below, busy picking among the cobblestones and horse-droppings, and explained the difference between them and homers, whilst the roast pork went cold and greasy. Then he sent for the waiter, complained about the food and managed to get some good roast beef in exchange!

This happy interlude did Gillespie's bile ducts so much

good that he said good-bye cordially to those whom he had hardly greeted when he entered, and when he got back to the police station he warmly commended certain officers for their diligence in a case they were handling.

"Gussie's got over it, thank God," said the constables to one another, and smiled and relaxed.

Gillespie's Christian names were Augustus Wilfred, by the way.

The inquest was quiet and precise. The Coroner, Mr. Emmanuel Querk, was tall, thin, and had a peculiar head. It was only a little broader than his long neck and ended in a point from which a fringe of downy grey hair spread like a curtain over his neck and ears. He wore old-fashioned spring pince-nez and looked very obstinate, which he was. He detested noise, had had double windows fitted to his court, and had given strict instructions that the usher was to eject anyone who made a sound. Every time anybody coughed, or even cleared his throat, Mr. Querk looked up and glared, a feat which put his head and neck in a constant state of agitation. A great hush, like that at a Quakers' meeting, pervaded the place, and this, added to the peculiar acoustics of the room, accentuated the noise of the witnesses.

Mr. Querk was County Coroner and had chosen to hold the inquest at his headquarters rather than at Hartsbury, where the presence of a sawmill right under the windows of the village hall frayed his nerves to such an extent that he was unable to concentrate on the work in hand.

Proceedings were brief with the exception of P.C. Puddiphatt's testimony, which he read from long sheets of paper apparently taken from the counter of the local butcher's shop. He had compiled this with the help of *The Policeman's Vade Mecum,* and was very proud of it, until Mr. Querk set about him for verbosity. But without his copy the village constable was hopeless, so the Coroner had to put up with it, which he did with the help of a number of bromide tablets, the taking of which caused him dreadful facial contortions.

Littlejohn listened carefully to the country bobby's rigmarole, and in his mind got a picture of what had happened. We have heard it all before and it would be sheer torture to go over it again in the form of Puddiphatt's official statement, copied in chunks from the *Vade Mecum* and suitably altered to suit the occasion, although there were parts where the constable had forgotten to amend the lines of his textbook to fit the case and he got a bit mixed up now and then and caused Mr. Querk to beat his brow and tear his hair.

There was a very useful line-up of other witnesses, too. Gillespie had certainly covered the ground well, if he had fallen short in finding a solution.

There was Mrs. Doakes, for example, dressed up to kill, and no mistake. Tweed skirt, scarlet coat, hat to match on the top of her peroxided head, and a diamond brooch, two diamond rings and a gold bracelet to set off the lot.

Mr. Querk's lack-lustre eyes fell upon her and he started and looked perturbed. Bright colours seemed to affect him the same as loud noises, and he kept averting his eyes from the red jacket as though it caused him intense pain.

Mrs. Doakes had been responsible for packing the box and getting it ready for transport.

"It was empty, I take it, at the time?"

Mr. Querk looked right over the top of Mrs. Doakes as he asked the question, and she was very annoyed about it. She wasn't used to men behaving as though she weren't there. On the contrary. . . .

"Certainly it was empty. And locked . . ."

"How did you know it was empty if it was locked?"

"I had to turn it about as I packed it. I'd have known if there'd been anything inside."

"Very good. You may step down. . . ."

Mrs. Doakes tossed her head and departed.

Then there was the man from the railway who had collected the box with his horse and lorry. His boots creaked and he was dressed in his best suit which he wore only for funerals and horse-shows. That morning he had taken three firsts and a special at Gosley Show and was a bit above himself. Each creak of the offending shoes might have been a dagger in Mr. Querk's heart, so badly did he take it.

"What are *you* looking so pleased about?" he peevishly asked the carter.

"Just taken three firsts and a special with my hosses at Gosley Show, sir . . ."

"Congratulations," surprisingly replied Mr. Querk, nobody knew why. The Coroner, however, was fond of horses. To him, they represented the quiet days before cars arrived to tear his nerves and take up his time with accident cases. . . .

The carter, red of face, burly of body and scrubbed until he shone again, added nothing to the case. He had merely gathered the box and taken it to the station for despatch on the train.

"It didn't seem unduly heavy?"

"No, sir. I managed to load it myself, signed for it, received the price and a small renumeration . . ."

"Remuneration?"

"Well, sir . . . Ahem, they usually . . ."

"Oh, I see. A tip. Yes, a tip . . ."

Nothing more.

Then the railway's officials.

The goods department remembered the box quite well. It hadn't seemed unduly heavy. They had loaded it in the van at the end of the London train, which would take it the first stage of its journey.

The guard then appeared. He was a loose-limbed, clumsy fellow, who fell on all-fours as he climbed into the witness-box, and Mr. Querk from his eminence above was seen to hold his brows and ears during the ensuing commotion, after which he drank water and chewed tablets again. A man with a cough at the back of the hall was ejected and the inquest went on.

Jeremiah Dimsdale, guard on the London train, testified that he had clipped a ticket for Mr. Grossman just after they left Fetling.

"Yes. It were a London ticket, sir."

"WAS a London ticket," wrote Mr. Querk, aloud.

"WAS a London ticket," repeated Jeremiah.

Small had already stated that his partner was on his way to London and had seemed quite himself when he left. Dimsdale confirmed that Mr. Grossman seemed quite merry and bright.

"Merry and bright," Mr. Querk was writing, and then he suddenly stopped. "Merry and bright?" he said gloomily. "Whatever is that?"

He knew very well, but he had taken a dislike to the noisy guard.

"Fit and well," modified the guard crisply.

"That's better."

"Did you see him again after you'd checked his ticket?"

"No, sir."

"Didn't that seem rather strange?"

"Well . . . Yes and no, sir."

"It can't be both. Yes *or* no?"

The guard, thus faced with a problem, said, "No."

"Why?"

"Well, you see, I went the woal length of the train. See? Then I stopped in the front van, checking stuff, like . . ."

"Like what?"

"Checkin' stuff. I forgets Mr. Gorssman, see?"

"I don't see, my man, but go on. . . ."

"An' I never gives 'im another thought. Maybe if I had, I'd just have thought he'd seen a friend and joined 'im in the more packed carriages at the front of the train. . . . You see, I can't keep tally of all and sundry on the train, sir. They used to 'ave a ticket collector as well as a guard on those trains, but now they's only a guard, see?"

"I DON'T SEE, but that will be enough," howled Mr. Querk. Whereupon Jeremiah retired, slipped down the steps of the box on his way back to his train, and left the Coroner in a state of nervous exhaustion.

"Owld Querk's as mad as an 'atter. Absolutely pots fer rags, 'e is," was what Jeremiah told his wife that night . . . or rather early the following morning when he returned from late duties.

"Never yew mind, Jeremiah," comforted his wife, who was as small and fat as he was long and thin. "It's 'is wife. Wore 'im out, she 'as, with 'er naggin' . . ."

Knowing Mr. Querk's idiosyncrasies, the jury, empanelled to assist him, had sat throughout the proceedings like a lot of stuffed dummies, hardly daring to move a muscle, take a note or turn a hair. One of them had sneezed and everybody had expected an eruption from the Coroner's pulpit. Instead, Mr. Querk had looked up from his notes and said "Bless you."

"Gettin' barmier and barmier," said the juryman afterwards. "They'll 'ave to put 'im away before long. Bless yer, indeed!"

The inquest was adjourned and Mr. Querk was glad to do it, for a hurdy-gurdy started in the street outside just as he was directing the jury and he could hardly wait for their verdict to beat a hasty retreat to his private room. There he locked the door, unlocked a cupboard and took out a bottle of whisky. It was all that stood between him and the complete madness to which his wife's endless debts and incessant nagging were driving him.

## 4

### THE MISSING KEY

THE fatal box was in a locked room in the Coroner's Court and after the inquest Gillespie took Littlejohn to see it.

It was just an ordinary chest. About two hundred or so years old and large enough comfortably to hold the body of a small man. It was carved in a kind of panelled Norman arches and ornamented with knops.

Now a funny thing arose. There was only one key to the box. And that had been in Miss Adlestrop's possession since she purchased it. She had paid for the chest in the shop, locked it possessively and carried away the key.

"But surely there are plenty of keys to fit a lock like this," said Littlejohn, squatting on his heels and examining the keyhole, set in a bed of wrought iron scrolls. He lifted the lid, too, and poked in the mechanism with his penknife.

Gillespie shook his head woefully. He sadly shrugged his shoulders and his long, sombre face grew even more sorrowful.

"You're welcome to try it, sir," he almost groaned. "I spent more than two hours yesterday with the best locksmith in the town trying keys. None would fit. Of course, to an expert locksmith the thing's chicken feed, if you get what I mean. But it's not a toy lock, I can assure you. Whoever made it intended only the rightful owner should get in that chest. And I took the trouble to enquire from the family about the keys. There's only been one in existence as long as Mr. Curwen had the box. . . ."

"No signs of forcing or prising, I see. . . ."

"No. Not a mark. And it couldn't have been Miss Adlestrop. She had the key in her handbag, which she took to the vicar's, playing whist all the time the crime was being committed. We checked that in every detail."

Littlejohn let the matter drop for the time being. Gillespie seemed disposed to believe that Grossman had got in the box by a conjuring trick! A sort of Harry Houdini murder!

Gillespie suggested that they pay another visit to the railway station, just to show Littlejohn how the matter had worked out. The Inspector was relieved, for he preferred to go over the ground itself rather than follow someone else's footsteps by means of an official report.

Fetling Station is rather a large one and assumes a certain importance in the summer season owing to weight of holiday-makers coming and going. Mr. Harry Fludd, the stationmaster, was, or fancied himself to be, a very important person. He thought himself worthy of a much higher post and had long awaited the time when he would change his peaked pancake hat for the tall-shiner of a real station mandarin. And here he was, still in Fetling, and only three years to retirement. It was a damned shame. He told his wife so, and she agreed. If Lord Trotwoode, the chairman of the company, would only travel by train instead of always running round in a Rolls Royce, he would encounter Mr. Fludd more often, realise his worth and promote him to a top hat at once. . . .

Mr. Fludd occupied an office almost like a lighthouse in Fetling Station. It was built over the refreshment room and an iron staircase led to it from Number One platform. There sat Mr. Fludd watching the trains come in and then watching them all go out and sending a runner down the iron staircase and rebuking him for slackness when he came back. He always descended himself to see the London, Manchester, Bristol and Birmingham trains off. In fact, anything with a corridor he deemed worthy of his attentions. . . .

Yes, he told his visitors, he himself had speeded the parting 7.45 p.m. train to London on the night of the murder.

Mr. Fludd conducted the interview seated at a plain wooden table in a bentwood armchair. He was tall, portly and bald. But to compensate for lack of hair on top, nature had endowed him with a magnificent red beard. It was like a flaming curtain over his collar and tie. In his young days Mr. Fludd had pursued painting as a hobby. The walls of his house up-town were covered almost from floor to ceiling with landscapes and still-lifes signed FLUDD in the bottom right corner, and his beard was all that was left of his early *vie Bohème*. Mrs. Fludd had married him on the strength of it. There must have been something aphrodisiac in that red beard, for ever after she would not hear of its removal. Or, perhaps, it reminded her of more carefree days, when Fludd was Fludd instead of a pompous luster for a top hat.

Littlejohn couldn't keep his eyes off the beard. He remembered his days on the beat when elderly, bearded gentlemen had implored his aid in dispersing bands of small boys who followed shouting gleefully in their wake. Here was one which would have delighted them. Beaver! Littlejohn almost shouted it himself.

"Yes, I saw the train out myself," foghorned Mr. Fludd at the two officers sitting uncomfortably on rickety wooden chairs, like spies being interrogated. "I spoke to Mr. Grossman. He said he was going to attend a sale of antiques by the 7.45, travelling overnight and returning late the following afternoon."

There were a number of indicators on the walls and these gave frequent reminders of their presence by the tinkle of little bells and the trembling of their needles. Every time a bell rang Mr. Fludd turned, looked at the relative dial, gave it a glare of contempt and returned to his task. There were buff forms, dirty files and large, dog-eared books on the table and stacks of correspondence on the floor.

"Mr. Grossman seemed all right . . . I mean in good spirits?" asked Littlejohn.

"Without a doubt; without a doubt," roared the station-master, and smoothed his beard.

"And now about the box—the oak chest. That went by passenger train?"

"Yes. Not the sort of thing I am accustomed to deal with. I leave that to subordinates. But in view of the trouble that 'as arisen, I have called for a full report. The box went by passenger train, well wrapped in the usual packing materials, and labelled *With Care* . . ."

"Which would make the men who handled it chuck it about a bit more than usual," giggled Gillespie biliously. He disliked Mr. Fludd and could not resist a little acid joke.

"I *beg* your pardon," thundered the beaver. The beard seemed to leap with flames and the poached, bloodshot eyes flashed.

"Did it travel on the same train with Mr. Grossman?" hastily said Littlejohn.

"Yes."

"In the baggage van?"

"In the luggage van, yes. To be delivered at Stainford Junction for the local to Hartsbury. I h'enquired from my colleague at Stainford. He tells me the chest was put off the express there and placed in the freight room, whence it was consigned to 'artsbury the following morning."

One of the indicators on the wall tinkled and the needle executed a violent dance. Mr. Fludd looked at it, read its cryptic message, and dismissed it with a frown.

"*The thrrree forty teeoo will depart for Creeoo from num-*

*ber thrrree pletfome. Orl steyshuns to Creeoo from nembah thrree pletfome . . .*" announced a magnified female voice in loud eddicated tones over the trumpets dotted here and there on the platforms below.

"So Grossman was probably killed on the train between Fetling and Stainton and put in the box on the way?"

"Doubtless. The chest was never out of sight after it reached Stainton. I 'ave the assurance of my colleague on that point. In view of the disgraceful pilfering going on, there's always somebody on duty watching the freight room there."

"And what about the guard on the train. I saw him at the inquest, but he was off before I could speak to him. Any chance of a word with him?"

Mr. Fludd rummaged among the papers on his desk, glared at them for not giving up their secrets promptly to him, pawed his beard and then took up a speaking tube down which he blew a wheezy blast.

"Oo was the guard on the 7.45 London, the day the man was murdered in the box?" he asked officiously. "Let me know quick."

"Dimsdale," said Gillespie.

Mr. Fludd glared at the Superintendent as though he didn't believe him and sat waiting for his answer from the other end of the contraption.

There was a loud whistle and Mr. Fludd uncorked the tube.

"Yes? Dimsdale? Right." He corked up again.

"I said so," said Gillespie.

"Dimsdale," rumbled Fludd to Littlejohn.

Gillespie's lips moved soundlessly under his small moustache.

"Could we have a word with him?" asked Littlejohn.

There was more uncorking and whistling.

"Yes. He's on the four o'clock London train."

The stationmaster consulted a huge timepiece which he drew from his pocket, and, as though doubting its integrity, also went to the window and glared at the station clocks.

"A little over twenty minutes. I'll get him. . . ."

Mr. Fludd rose, pressed a switch, and spoke.

"Guard Dimsdale of the four o'clock train to London will please report at the stationmaster's office . . . Guard Dimsdale . . ."

*"Gawd Dimsdeyle uf the faw o'cluck treyn to Lenden will please reepawt et the steyshunmestah's offiss. Gawd Dimsdeyle . . ."* roared all the loud-speakers on the platforms.

There were sounds of scuffling below, and footsteps began to climb the iron staircase, trotting, fumbling and apparently falling up every other step.

"Wot the 'ell? Oh . . ."

The loose-limbed, tall, hairy guard appeared in the doorway. He apparently wasn't enamoured of Fludd, but the three of them rather overfaced him.

"Dimsdale, these two gentlemen are from the police. They want a word or two with you . . ."

"Uhu," said Dimsdale to the stationmaster. He knew he had his Union at the back of him, so treated Fludd without respect. He smiled upon Littlejohn, however.

"I know you've already testified at the inquest, Mr. Dimsdale . . ."

That was better. *Mister* Dimsdale. The guard bared his long teeth in approval and cantered up to Littlejohn in his eagerness to be of use. He removed his cap even, revealing thin, black hair plastered down firmly and a curly quiff across his brow which looked to be rigidly held in place by glue.

"Yuss?"

"You saw Grossman board the train here?"

"Right you are, sir."

"And you clipped his ticket?"

"Yuss. He were alone in a fust-class, see? Three doors from my van at the back it was."

"Corridor train all the way?"

"Yes. All London trains are corridor," interposed Mr. Fludd.

"Yuss," said Dimsdale, as though the stationmaster hadn't spoken.

"What were your movements about that time, guard?"

"I started to go through the train . . ."

"What time would that be?"

"About seven-fifty. Just after we'd cleared the station and yards here . . ."

"Yes?"

"I went through the train and clipped tickets."

"Including Grossman's?"

"Yuss. Quite merry and bright, he were."

"*Was*," groaned the beaver.

"*Were*," repeated the guard. No nonsense from Fludd.

" 'Nice night. 'ope we 'ave a good trip', sez he to me. 'No reason why not', I sez, and then gets along."

"When did you reach the front?"

"Oh, about ten past eight. Yes, I looked at me watch. We was due in Stainford at 8.15 . . ."

"*Were* due . . ."

"*Was*. Was due at 8.15 and was runnin' to time."

"And you stayed at the front till you reached Stainton?"

"Yuss. Doin' odd jobs, like. Lookin' to see if we'd anythin' to put off at Stainton . . ."

"I see."

"And you saw the chest put off at Stainton?"

"Yuss. Told a coupla men there as it were for the 'artsbury local, so they tuck it and carried it to the goods office."

"Did they pass any remarks about the weight of it?"

"I weren't there when they lifted it. I was busy with the train."

"So, in your absence, it looks as though Grossman was hit over the head and put in the box. . . . Summing up, then: Grossman and the chest on the train at 7.45, or thereabouts . . ."

"Right," said Mr. Fludd.

"Yuss," concurred Dimsdale.

"At 7.50 you, guard, passed down the train, saw Grossman, and then left the coast clear till 8.15, when you reached Stainford, where the box was removed. Between these times the crime seems to have been committed. Did you see anything suspicious going on, guard?"

"No. The corridors isn't lighted yet . . ."

"*Aren't,*" pleaded Fludd.

"*Isn't.* The black-out's over, but they haven't yet put back the lamps. Whether they've been lost on the station . . ."

"Stick to the point, Dimsdale," roared Fludd.

"Lost on the station . . . The people in the two compartments between my van and Mr. Gorssman's one was strangers. Didn't know 'em from Adam. Prob'ly going home from 'olidays . . ."

"And the rest?"

"Same on the other side. You see, locals goin' to London get the mornin' train as a rule. Don't wanter travel overnight. But 'oliday people like to stop on as long as they can and don't mind the night trip at times."

"So you can't call to mind anybody else prominent locally?"

"No. To-in' and from-in' like I do, I fergets 'em, like. No, I can't recollect . . ."

Mr. Fludd blew through his red beard. *He* would have remembered. You have to be smart and perspicacious if you aspire to a top-hat.

"Did you take a good look at the chest, guard?"

"Yuss. Looked at the label. Miss Somebody-or-other, 'artsbury. I do remember that. Orl I wanted to know wuzz where I got to put it off."

"It was wrapped in sacking and stitched?"

"Yuss. I remember that, too."

Gillespie interposed.

"Yes. A sort of large bag with the open top gathered or roughly sewn together. Mrs. Doakes says she fastened it securely herself with string threaded through a packing-needle. We didn't get so far, with the inquest being adjourned, but we found the string on the floor of the van, didn't we, Dimsdale?"

"Yuss . . ."

"Whoever killed Grossman stitched up the cover again, roughly, with black cotton . . ."

"Ah! Must have been prepared for it," suggested Littlejohn.

"Looks like it."

The loudspeakers were barking again.

*"The faw o'clock treyn, express to Lenden, will deepawt frum pletfawm faw . . . Pletfawm faw, Lenden express . . ."*

"Want me any more?" anxiously asked the guard.

Fludd, too, was on his feet. He had the train to Lenden to see off. Lord Trotwoode might . . . If the Rolls Royce happened to crack-up, which it never did . . .

"I suppose you've both your duties to attend to," said Littlejohn. "Thank you very much for your help. We'll be getting along."

Dimsdale hurried out without another word and could be heard falling down the iron staircase in his haste to get back to his faw o'clock.

Mr. Fludd put on his official cap, shrugged his jacket into its proper place on his shoulders, removed a stray piece of cotton from his pants and combed his beard into symmetry. Then he inspected the result in a looking-glass on the wall. The needles in several indicators began to dance frenziedly to the accompaniment of little bells.

Mr. Fludd led the way downstairs. It was like a royal procession. He left them at the barriers of pletfawm faw.

"Any fingerprints on the box?" asked Littlejohn as they passed the newspaper stall.

"None on the inside. That fool of a village constable, Pruddifatt or something, moved the body and let the charwoman polish the box up. Outside, the thing was so messed up we couldn't get a clear print of any kind. There seemed to be what might have been Grossman's, Small's, Mrs. Doakes's and Miss Adlestrop's . . . Lot of unidentified ones, too. Scores of people would have handled a thing like that . . . On sale publicly. Like hunting for a needle in a haystack."

"Yes . . ."

*"The Lenden treyn is about chew depawt from pletfawm faw. Pessengahs faw the Gossley, Hawtsberry lane, cheynge at Steynfud. Lenden express deepawts at faw frum pletfawm faw . . ."*

Littlejohn looked back from the exit. The fiery beaver could be seen triumphantly flaming about the middle of the train. Lord Trotwoode's car was in dock at last and he had turned up like an answer to a stationmaster's prayer!

## 5

### MOTIVE?

"WHAT about motive?"

The two police officers were on their way back to the police station after interviewing Mr. Fludd. Gillespie seemed to be imparting the background of the crime on the instalment plan and Littlejohn was developing an itch to have the reins of the case in his fingers and go off on his own gathering background, as was his custom.

"None, as far as I can see. Grossman hadn't much ready cash on him and such as he had was intact. He'd his cheque book and a gold watch as well, untouched."

"Not robbery, then."

"I'd say not. Harmless little chap, too. No enemies that I can find. Too innocuous. The actual smothering may, of course, have been an accident. Somebody may have tried to rob him, laid him out, and been disturbed before they could search him. So dumped him in the chest . . ."

"Even then, what about stitching up the sacking again?"

"That might have been done when the alarm was past."

"Looks queer, all the same."

Gillespie lapsed into melancholy silence again. He changed step to keep in time with his companion. He had very heavy boots and they rang like iron on the pavement. Tramp, tramp, tramp, the boys are marching . . .

"What about the relations between Grossman and Small, Gillespie?"

"Seemed to get on all right with both Small and Mrs. Doakes. He'd no vices, either, as far as we can gather. Didn't even smoke or drink."

Littlejohn parked his colleague at the police station, where Gillespie had matters to attend to, and he made his way to *The Seven Whistlers* alone. Both Small and Mrs. Doakes were in the shop.

Small was so flabbily fat that he looked to be trundling his paunch before him like a railway-porter wheeling baggage about. He was smoking a black cheroot which he kept removing from his mouth and then replacing with a repulsive movement of his lips, like a hungry child taking the teat of a feeding-bottle.

"Who'd want to do Isidore in? Harmless enough, wasn't he, Doris?" he said in answer to Littlejohn's question.

Small looked across the shop at the blonde woman standing at the trinket counter. She was busy with a soldier who was buying some knick-knack or other, and giving him all she'd got in the way of sex-appeal. It seemed to leave the soldier cold.

"Mild as milk," was her indifferent reply.

The soldier gave her a funny glance.

Littlejohn nodded. He didn't like the looks of either Small or Mrs. Doakes.

"I believe you were in charge of the antique furniture side of the business, Mr. Small. Did the box in which Mr. Grossman's body was found pass through your hands?"

"Nope. Mr. Grossman bought it himself at the sale. Paid too much for it in my opinion. I was a bit huffed about the way he did it. So I washed my hands of it and told him to get what he'd paid for it, if he could. He managed to sell it for a small profit."

"Did you examine the box?"

Small passed a big hand across his sloppy lips, spat out some bits of tobacco, replaced his cheroot and spoke round it.

"Nope. It arrived one afternoon, and the following morning, as soon as we opened, the woman came in and bought it."

"They tell me it belonged to a Mr. Curwen, who died. Where could I find any of his family, executors, or such like?"

"His only daughter, Barbara, lives at the house. I hear she's soon leaving town. They've sold off all the stuff she doesn't want and she's taken a smaller house somewhere else."

"What's her present address?"

"Laurieston, Beech Avenue. Last street at the end of the promenade. You can't miss it . . ."

"Thanks. So you've no suggestions as to why anybody should want to do Mr. Grossman any harm?"

Small removed his ragged cheroot again. He looked hard at Littlejohn and then thrust his face close to the Inspector's.

"Nope," he said hoarsely.

"He was on his way to an auction in London at the time. Did he go frequently?"

"About twice in three months, as a rule. But, if there were any important sales advertised, he'd go specially as well. This was his usual routine visit."

"Had he anything valuable with him which your firm wanted to sell?"

"Not a thing."

"Where did he stay as a rule?"

"Good God! How many more questions? I've work to do."

He didn't look as if he had much, or if he had, he didn't look like settling down to it!

"The address, please."

"Ridgfields' Hotel, off the Haymarket. Quiet family place. He's been going there for years."

"Where were *you* between eight and nine on the night Mr. Grossman died, Mr. Small?"

The dealer's piggy little eyes flickered and he gave Littlejohn a dirty look.

"You're not thinking that I . . . ?"

"Not at all. A routine enquiry. Where were you?"

"It'd better only be routine, too. It might be bad for you to make insinuations of that sort . . ."

And Mr. Small laughed, a neighing, mirthless laugh, apparently at the thought of how bad it would be for Littlejohn.

"Well?"

"I was in the lounge of the Bay Hotel. The waiters and a lot of other regulars'll confirm that. You needn't waste your time tryin' to pin this on me."

"Thanks."

The soldier had by this time made up his mind not to buy anything and was gone. There was nobody else in the shop, so Littlejohn repeated his question to Mrs. Doakes.

"Me?" she asked, as though astonished at the Inspector's impudence. "Me? What should I be doing murdering anybody?"

"That's not the point, Mrs. Doakes. Please answer."

She tossed her head and pursed her lips. Then she boldly looked Littlejohn in the face and her squint became more manifest.

"At the pictures . . ."

"Which?"

"*The Palace,* on the prom."

"Anyone with you?"

"No."

Littlejohn knew by the way it was said that she was lying.

Probably she'd got herself some boy friend or other and didn't want the relationship too closely investigated.

"Not very helpful, are you, Mrs. Doakes?"

"What do you mean?"

"It's in your own interest to clear yourself . . ."

She put her hands on her hips and looked Littlejohn up and down as bold as brass.

"You've got a nerve!"

"Think it over, Mrs. Doakes. I'll be seeing you again."

Littlejohn made his exit decidedly of the opinion that he'd outstayed his welcome at *The Seven Whistlers*. Small and his niece stood glaring at him and trying to brazen it out, but they didn't look too comfortable about it all. . . .

It was about teatime, but Littlejohn felt he would like to see Hartsbury and some of the people present when Mr. Grossman arrived there in his improvised coffin. He sought out *The Saracen's Head* again, where Gillespie had fixed up a room for him, trotted round the revolving door, had afternoon tea and a quiet smoke, trotted into the street again and caught the 'bus for Hartsbury.

P.C. Puddiphatt, Miss Adlestrop and Councillor Blanket were the main characters at the Hartsbury end, and Blanket had taken charge when the constable's powers and initiative gave out.

Mr. Blanket, the 'bus conductor informed him, lived in a bungalow on the outskirts of the village. You couldn't miss it. The 'bus passed the door and he'd show Littlejohn. He'd find old Blanket in a good temper, because he'd come out top of the poll at the council elections yesterday.

There were noises like a wild west rodeo going on in Hartsbury when Littlejohn turned up. He wondered whatever was the matter. Shots, cheering and the thudding of hooves. He had not time to investigate, but turned-in at the bungalow occupied by Councillor Blanket and his housekeeper.

There was nobody at home, but a passing bread-boy informed the Inspector that Mr. Blanket was celebrating his recent victory at the Rural District elections by officiating at the village sports. He had also provided buns and coffee as a thank-offering for his recent triumph over the local Bolshie.

Following the directions of the boy, who, to show his irritation at having to work whilst everybody else was sporting on the green, tossed the loaves about contemptuously with dirty hands and even dropped a few in the nearby ditch and rescued them in a shocking condition, Littlejohn came upon the scene of the revels.

The large field was crowded with men, women and children. The women were in their best and gayest whilst the men wore the funereal hats, suits and boots which countrymen love to assume on occasions of public jollification. There was a temporary hush, for the contestants were about to start two of the heats.

Councillor Blanket was in charge of one of the running-tracks; the Rev. Mellodew Gryper, M.A. (Oxon.), the vicar, the other. There were events of all kinds, from twenty yards for babes and sucklings to a hundred and twenty yards egg-and-spoon for veterans.

Mr. Gryper was the starter for the toddlers, the sack race, the open events for men and women over forty, and the junior boys' three-legged canter.

Mr. Blanket took the rest. He bullied and handicapped the junior and senior boys. He almost boxed the ears of the adolescent youths. He jested heavily with the women over forty (egg-and-spoon, threading-the-needle, and trimming-the-hat races), and took a particular interest in the young ladies over fifteen (100 yards flat) whom he fondly placed in their due positions and then, for many of them were dressed in shorts, he assumed a pair of glasses the better to see that they did not cheat.

Mr. Blanket, of course, started them off with a pistol.

"Get ready! Get set!!" BANG.

There was a scuffle of feet, yells of encouragement, groans and then another bang. The latter due to a patent of Mr. Alfred Adlestrop, which detonated a sort of grenade when the winner breasted the tape.

The vicar, a man of peace, released his squads with a handkerchief.

"One. Two. Three. Away!"

Mr. Gryper had a voice like an oboe, and it broke as he called the final word.

"No! No! No! Come back. I didn't say *Away* . . ."

"One. Two. Three. AWAY . . .!"

The noise was not so clear as in Mr. Blanket's crisp events.

Shuffle-shuffle, bumpity-bump, went the sack and three-legged runners. Then BANG, as another of Uncle Alfred's whizz-bangs went up in smoke.

Uncle Alfred was at the other end, running between the two finishing tapes, fixing his infernal machines and dancing like a wild Indian on the warpath as they went off. There was too much bombardment for some of the younger runners, who either stopped half way down the track and started to scream, or else, just before touching the tape, turned on their heels in terror of the salute to come and ran back to Mr. Blanket, who brandished his pistol, or to the vicar who was shouting encouragement, impartially, of course, to one and another of the struggling mass he had one-two-three and Awayed.

"One. Two. Three. Away . . . ! Good, good, Ethel. Come along, Alice. Oh, what a shame, Bertha. On, on, you're winning. Ohhhhh," he oboed, trying to urge them all on without fear or favour. He sounded at times as though somebody were murdering him, and his contortions suggested that someone might have dropped a wasps' nest down his pants.

Between them, Mr. Blanket with his revolver and Mr. Gryper yelling his head off, they looked like two protagonists in an old-time melodrama.

Nobody seemed to have any time for Littlejohn and his murder. He thought it unwise to disturb the Councillor until he had blasted off all the contestants, so sat smoking and sunning himself on a bench until the recess for food. It was very pleasant. The sun was hot, the scenery soothing and the atmosphere one of goodwill and jollity. Littlejohn pulled his hat down over his eyes and relaxed.

The heats were finally finished. Mr. Blanket, pistol still in hand and a preposterous bowler on his head, was encouraging the young ladies, telling them how to win next time, and still wearing his glasses. The vicar, palpitating with excitement and exhaustion, was congratulating the winners, wishing everybody luck without fear or favour, and commiserating with the losers with a sort of holy gusto. A starter of heats for the kingdom of heaven's sake!

Uncle Alfred was sitting among his detonators and smiling like a baby who has just spotted the bottle.

All the heats were over. The finals were on the morrow, with more buns and ginger pop from the successful councillor.

Mr. Blanket, Mr. Gryper and Uncle Alfred foregathered for consultations . . . One in his ridiculous bowler, a symbol of some sort or another, probably Freud could have told him what. The vicar in his shovel hat, making reaping gestures with his arms. The harvest was truly great and the labourers few . . . And then Uncle Alfred wearing his straw boater which looked to be made of breakfast cereal.

"The handicapping for the young ladies' race . . . just a little bit too easy for the larger girls, don't you think, sir?"

Councillor Blanket towered over the vicar like a furious John Bull after the lion's tail had been tweaked. But, by jingo, if we do . . .!!!

"Vicar!!! I've been handicapping these past forty years . . ."

That was enough. The vicar caved-in. He scythed apologetically with his hands. He'd made his stand and satisfied his conscience.

> Dare to be a Daniel,
> Dare to stand alone,
> Dare to have a purpose firm,
> And dare to make it known.

He'd made it known . . .

It was no use. He couldn't stand up to Mr. Blanket. He blinked his charred eyelids over tired eyes, and his snouty little nose twitched. Blanket ruled the roost . . . In the name of Blanket, Amen . . . !

Littlejohn approached the trio.

"Councillor Blanket?"

"Yes. What can I do for you?"

John Bull looked ready to defend himself to the last drop of blood.

Uncle Alfred led the vicar off.

"Now, if we could have two detonators instead of one to-morrow. First and second at the tape . . . You see . . ."

Their voices died away, the vicar oboeing agreement.

Buns and coffee were being served. There was a scramble for food before supplies gave out. Sam Biles, the porter, had called for a free feed between trains. A widow with designs on him had given him a hard-boiled egg to eat with his buns and the yolk festooned his beard like decorations on a Christmas tree.

Littlejohn's card knocked the stuffing out of Councillor Blanket at first. He looked to have shrunk in the wash. He thought they were on his track for corrupt practices at the election. After all, surely the promise of two days' buns and coffee at the sports couldn't be regarded . . .

He perked up, however, when he heard the purpose of the Inspector's visit.

"Very willin' to help, I'm sure. But I haven't much time. You see, there's dancing after tea and I'm in charge of events . . ."

Councillor Blanket wasn't going to miss the dancing. Oh, no. He was going to hop and skip over the sward with the rest of them to the strains of the Fetling Town Band. With the help of his glasses at the heats, he'd already made a mental list of partners.

". . . Perhaps it'd be as well if we went over to Miss Adlestrop's cottage. She could tell her story as well and I could show you just how things happened."

"That would be fine. Shall we go?"

"Yes . . . Just a minute . . ."

Mr. Blanket dived into the crowd milling for food round the tea tent.

He handed a large bottle of pillules to the woman in charge. Hundreds of doses of a ten-thousandth of a grain of *Arnica*! *Similia similibus curantur* . . .

"If any of you feel stiff with runnin', or have overdone it a bit, take three pills from the bottle."

"And now let's be off."

Taking Littlejohn by the elbow he propelled him at great speed in the direction of Miss Adlestrop's house, like Virgil hustling Dante along and giving him no time to pause and question the damned.

Behind them, two violent explosions shook the air as Uncle Alfred showed the vicar what he meant. Young children started to howl and the rooks in the vicarage trees all rose in dismay with wild cawing.

*  6  *

## THE RIVALS

MR. BLANKET peeped impudently through the window of Miss Adlestrop's cottage as he and Littlejohn made their way to the front door.

"What the hell's *he* doing here?" asked the Councillor, and recoiled in distaste. His face flushed and the back of his neck grew almost black with temper.

Inside, they found Miss Adlestrop in earnest conversation with a small, portly man who looked like a pug dog with George Robey eyebrows.

"This is Mr. Troyte, Inspector," explained the lady after Mr. Blanket had introduced the pair of them and huffily explained the purpose of their visit. The Councillor ignored Mr. Troyte, except that he gave him a perforating glare.

"Deelighted to meet you . . . Deelighted," said Mr. Troyte. He had a pug dog's teeth, as well, and his voice came from straight behind them, a sort of wuffing noise, thick and unctuous. Like one of Walt Disney's large, benevolent animals. It gave you a queer sort of feeling when he gave tongue. As though a pet dog suddenly started to articulate.

Miss Adlestrop looked a bit sheepish. Littlejohn wondered if these two pompous friends of the little old maid were rivals for her hand, but soon found he was wrong. They were antagonists in a higher cause. They carried on a perpetual battle for Miss Adlestrop's very good health.

Littlejohn and his murder again faded temporarily into the background.

"How are you, Selina?" asked Blanket in challenging tones.

"I am very well, thank you," replied the little lady with a trace of uneasiness.

Mr. Troyte washed his hands in thin air and looked very pleased. He was a Christian Scientist and had been giving Miss Adlestrop half-an-hour's work-out just before the Inspector and his companion broke in upon them.

"There is no illness . . Only error, shpirichool error . ." he wuffed. "Breath is Life . . ."

He had tacked a theory of correct breathing to the established doctrine and looked as if he practiced what he preached. His pug's nostrils were wide as though from continual deep inhaling and he looked to have blown his teeth half-way out of his gums by vigorously exhaling through his lips.

"Breath is Life . . ."

Mr. Blanket ignored him.

"Did you take the medicine?" asked Mr. Blanket stiffly, suspiciously eyeing an empty tumbler on the table. He had been giving her *Ignatia* for the nerve shock of the murder.

"Some of it," replied Miss Adlestrop.

"Some of it . . . ?" thundered Mr. Blanket.

"*I* poured the remainder on the geranium," barked Mr. Troyte, and set himself for the impact of an attack. "There is no illness . . . Only shpirichool error . . ."

Councillor Blanket looked at the geranium on the window sill as though expecting it to turn from red to blue at any moment.

"Spirichool Rubbish!!" he thundered. "I'll ask you to stop

callin' here with your Error and your Breath and stuffing your nonsense into my friend . . ."

Mr. Troyte continued to grin. He was breathing deeply and muttering words of control inwardly. Inhale . . . Exhale . . . There is no Anger . . . Shpirichool Error . . .

This business had been going on in desultory fashion for months and Miss Adlestrop wouldn't make up her mind between Like Cures Like . . . *similia similibus curantur* . . . and Shpirichool Error.

It looked as though battle to the death were to be joined between Hahnemann and Mrs. Eddy.

Littlejohn intervened. He was fed up with it all.

"Excuse me," he said. "I want to talk to Miss Adlestrop for a minute or two. Would you two gentlemen mind finishing your argument in the garden?"

Miss Adlestrop looked greatly relieved.

"Yes, yes," she said, and, hurrying over to Littlejohn, stood by his side as though seeking protection from a neutral.

"I've really nothing more to say," wuffed Mr. Troyte. It was like the noise a dog makes in his dreams; a muffled barking.

"GOOD!" thundered Blanket. "Good job! For when you say it, it's all tommy rot . . ."

"One can lead a man to the waters of life, but one cannot make him drink . . . I hope one day, sir, you'll see your shpirichool error . . . Your eyes will be opened . . . Good day, Miss Adlestrop . . . Good-bye, Inspector . . . Remember, dear lady, Breath is Life . . ." Disneyed Mr. Troyte as Miss Adlestrop showed him out. He bounced down the garden path, turning to bare his fangs in what was supposed to be a benedictive grin.

"And now I'll mix you some more and see you take it all this time. No more of Troyte and his poppycock."

Mr. Blanket beat a retreat into the kitchen to mix his

potions and Littlejohn got on with the job in hand. The atmosphere of the place was very restful, especially after the medical battle which had just fizzled out. It was a pity to talk murder there.

"It's about the death of Mr. Grossman, Miss Adlestrop. I'm sorry to bring up a subject which I'm sure has distressed you, but I must do so."

"Quite right, Inspector Littlejohn. I wish to help all I can. Such a nice man, and so gentle and polite. It was horrible."

She scuttered to a drawer in the sideboard, produced a bottle of smelling salts, took a good sniff, recoiled from their potency and seemed better for it.

"You knew Mr. Grossman very well?"

"Yes. From dealing with him, you know. I spend quite a lot of time at Fetling on holiday. I always call at *The Seven Whistlers*. I've bought a lot of very nice stuff there."

She indicated a cabinet full of cut-glass, and Dresden, Chelsea and Staffordshire ornaments scattered about the room.

"You knew Mr. Small and Mrs. Doakes, too, I take it?"

"Yes . . . I didn't much care for them, though. I always dealt with Mr. Grossman. He was a gentleman."

"Why didn't you like the other two?"

"Mr. Small was common, and he drinks. So unaccommodating, too. It seemed too much trouble for him to bother with you."

"And Mrs. Doakes?"

"I thought her common, too. Didn't seem interested in selling anything to women. She was always occupied with men—selling souvenirs and such like, and talking familiarly to them, if you understand what I mean?"

"I do, Miss Adlestrop. And do you think the three of them got on well together?"

"Oh, yes. They always seemed to. Sometimes I thought Mr. Small and Mrs. Doakes made a jest of Mr. Grossman. I have caught them making gestures and smiling behind his back at times, as though enjoying a private joke. I suppose they were more intimate with each other than with Mr. Grossman. They live together on the premises and are relatives. Mr. Grossman lived elsewhere."

"Yes, so I hear. Now, as regards the box. Did anything about the purchase strike you as funny at the time?"

"Nothing whatever, Inspector Littlejohn."

"You had the key, I understand, and gave it up to Superintendent Gillespie. Was there only one key?"

"That is all. It was in the lock when I bought it in the shop, and, thinking it might be lost in transit, I took it as I paid for the box, put it in my handbag and there it remained until the box was delivered here on that dreadful day. I used it to open the box and . . ."

Here she took another mighty sniff at the smelling-salts and opened her mouth, closed her eyes and raised her eyebrows in a struggle to recover from the fumes.

"You had it in your handbag all the time between putting it there in the shop and taking it out when the box arrived from the station?"

"Certainly, Inspector. And as Mr. Grossman assured me they hadn't another key, I've been terribly worried to know how his body got in the box. How was it opened when I had the only key? I'm sure I locked it before I left the shop. I shook the lid to make sure."

"Yes, it's quite a mystery. But there must be a simple solution somewhere. We must find it."

Councillor Blanket entered, carrying a glass of his precious medicine.

"Here you are, Selina. And see you take it proper this time. Tablespoonful every two hours, and no more Troyte."

"Thank you, Mr. Blanket."

"I wonder if you'd mind taking a turn in the garden, sir," suggested Littlejohn. "We're just in the middle of an important discussion."

"Oh, if I'm not wanted I'll take myself off. Plenty to do on the sports-ground. Dancin' begins soon."

"Please don't be annoyed, Mr. Blanket," pleaded Miss Adlestrop, anxious not to be cruel. "I will take your medicine, and thank you so much for your kindly thought."

Councillor Blanket perked up and smiled.

"And when you've finished with your murder, Selina, come across to the field, if you like. There's a band there. Come and trip the light fantastic a bit. Take you out of yourself and help you to forget your spirichool errors . . ."

And, with this heavy sally, Councillor Blanket bade his friend *au revoir,* gave Littlejohn a curt nod and went off to trip and trot on the village green. Miss Adlestrop blushed and lowered her eyes.

"Now, madam, can you tell me exactly what happened when the box arrived?"

Miss Adlestrop fixed her eyes on a distant point through the window, like a sibyl about to prophesy.

"It's quite simple, really. The men from the station arrived with the chest. I had a number of friends present and wanted them all to see my bargain. So I told Biles, the porter, to bring the box in here. He put it down just there . . ."

Miss Adlestrop indicated the exact spot on the carpet where he put it.

". . . I took the scissors and unfastened the wrapping . . ."

"It was hessian, I believe. A sort of large bag stitched at the top . . ."

"That is right, Inspector. I see you know all about it."

"You cut the stitching at the top. What was it like?"

"I remember remarking how poorly it was done. In black cotton instead of proper twine or such. It might easily have broken away."

"Yes. Mrs. Doakes says she fastened it with carpet thread and a packing needle."

"So . . ."

The horrible truth dawned on Miss Adlestrop and she brought the smelling-salts to her assistance again.

"Please go on with your account, Miss Adlestrop."

"Well, we removed the covering and I took a duster and lightly wiped off the dust outside."

"Ah!"

"Yes. I'm so sorry. Inspector Gillespie made a similar noise when I told him. But I didn't know there was a—a—Mr. Grossman was inside and that fingerprints would be important, you see. Mr. Gillespie was most annoyed, I remember. It took him all his time to speak civilly . . . And he was more annoyed than ever with Mrs. Hollis and poor Puddiphatt."

"What about?"

"Well, you see, when we opened the box and found—and found—Mr. Grossman, it was such a shock that I went completely over. I didn't remember anything else for some time after—after—Mr. Grossman—after . . ."

"I understand."

"They sent straight away for Puddiphatt, who came with Mr. Hale. Poor Mr. Hale fainted, too, and has been in bed ever since. Puddiphatt took the body out of the box. I don't quite know why he did it, but Mr. Gillespie was furious. They say he raised his hand to strike poor Puddiphatt, who is now so distressed that he's told one or two of the villagers that he's contemplating taking his own life."

"Dear me!"

"Yes. And whilst the constable was dealing with Mr.

Grossman—poor Puddiphatt was only trying to revive him, although I believe the body was quite cold—whilst he was ministering to the body on the rug, Mrs. Hollis, my charlady, came in and polished the inside of the box with furniture cream. To take away the smell of death, she said. Poor Mr. Gillespie was really ill when he heard. He beat himself on the top of his head with his clenched fist and swore horribly. Mrs. Hollis said her only regret was that she didn't work for him, then she could give notice at once and leave him in the lurch . . ."

"I can understand Superintendent Gillespie's feelings, Miss Adlestrop. You see, Mrs. Hollis rubbed out any fingerprints that may have been in the box. Not that they'd have made much difference. I don't lay much store by that sort of thing myself. But please don't mention my tastes outside . . ."

"Of course not."

"Was there anything inside the box besides the body?"

"Not that I've heard. And I'm sure Mrs. Hollis would have told me if she found anything when she cleaned it."

"Is she here now?"

"I'm afraid not. It's rather late. She said she was going to Fetling to see her married daughter this afternoon, so I don't think you'll find her in if you call at her house. She lives at the row of little cottages opposite the village stores. You know where that is? Well . . . the second house from this end."

"Thank you very much. I'd like just a word with her some time. Could I get her to-morrow?"

"Yes. She should be here in the afternoon until five o'clock."

"Thank you. And now I must be going."

"Florence is making you a cup of tea . . ."

Outside, the weather had suddenly changed. The sky was overcast and what looked like a thunderstorm was blowing up. The sky over Fetling, however, looked clear, and shafts of sunshine poured down like something almost solid.

There was a flash of lightning, and Uncle Alfred, wearing his breakfast-cereal hat, appeared with his arms full of detonators and other contraptions. He was so eager to get them under cover in his hut that he hadn't time to stop at the house, but scuttered down to his lair at the bottom of the garden and vanished through the door.

The band could be heard playing for The Lancers on the village green. Councillor Blanket always insisted on The Lancers.

There was a peal of thunder like the emptying of a cartload of mighty paving stones. Then the rain came.

It kept Littlejohn immobilised at Miss Adlestrop's for nearly an hour. The sun continued to shine over Fetling. Peal followed peal of thunder, and from the bottom of the garden could be heard explosions in between those of the elements as Uncle Alfred experimented with his whizz-bangs for the morrow. He had promised to give a firework display after the races.

The falling rain, the eerie sky dappled with heavy cloud and distant sunshine, and the streams of sodden, dishevelled villagers rushing home, made Littlejohn think of the Cities of the Plain receiving their dues . . .

Miss Adlestrop showed Littlejohn all the bargains in cut-glass and ornaments she had bought at *The Seven Whistlers*. The display cabinet was a choice piece, supplied, she said, by Mr. Grossman. And then she gave a little scream.

Sacrilegiously and defiantly plunged into the shelf above the glass doors and in front of a pretty Dresden figure was a pin surmounted by a small flag.

"Who could have put that there?" said Miss Adlestrop, angrily removing the offending object.

"Is that the first you've seen of it, Miss Adlestrop?"

"Yes—I can't think—It wasn't there—Let me see—The last time it was dusted was before the meeting when the box came. We've been so upset since. I don't know . . ."

"And you're sure you haven't seen it before and that it wasn't there when Grossman's body arrived?"

"Quite sure."

"H'm. I'll take it with me, if you please. It may be nothing, but I'd better keep it."

"By all means. Although I don't see the connection."

"Nor do I at present. When was the flag-day, do you remember?"

"I'm sorry, I couldn't say. It wasn't held whilst I was in Fetling and there wasn't one in Hartsbury . . . No, I can't help you, Inspector."

"Thank you, all the same. And I'm very grateful to you for all your help and for the refreshment, Miss Adlestrop."

The rain had ceased. There was a 'bus due in ten minutes, so Littlejohn bade Miss Adlestrop good-bye and made his way to the centre of the village.

The band was finishing its day in the village hall, which vibrated from the dancing of those who had managed to keep dry. The large, red face of Councillor Blanket rotated past one of the windows as he cavorted with one of the pretty girls of the place. He saw Littlejohn, but pretended not to. . . .

## 7

### MARK CURWEN'S BOX

A BOLD-LOOKING maid with good looks which would probably one day lead her into trouble, opened the door of Laurieston to Littlejohn.

"Miss Curwen's out, but should be back any time. Would you care to wait?"

The house was higgledy-piggledy from preparations for removal, but the maid took Littlejohn to a moderately tidy room, albeit the pictures had been removed from the walls, leaving light patches where they had been hanging. The whole place was bare of ornaments.

At the front door stood a large pantechnicon.

HOAR AND COMPANY
*Furniture Removers*
*By Road, Rail or Sea.*

In neighbouring rooms you could hear the removers' men busy at the job. They sounded to be taking the furniture to pieces to get it out and were banging and hammering as though in a frenzy.

Now and then there was a scuffling sound, and two grey-headed workers and a young one with a cigarette hanging from the corner of his mouth appeared, carried a sideboard or a table down the weed-grown drive and dumped it in the van without any ceremony.

"I suppose you'll soon be out of a job, if Miss Curwen's removing."

Littlejohn was sitting smoking on a packing-case, hoping that Miss Curwen wouldn't be long.

The maid tossed her head.

"Plenty more, *and* better. I shan't be long out of a place."

She sniggered as though challenging Littlejohn to deny it.

"How long have you been here?"

"Long enough. Five years."

"Like it?"

"So so. It was all right when Mr. Mark was alive. A good master, he was. Miss Barbara's a bit short and snappy. Specially since Mr. Mark died. A change'll do me good."

"Do you remember the oak box that was sold by auction recently?"

"The one the body was put in? Coo, rather! Dusted it many a time. I little thought when I was doin' it that . . ."

"Yes, yes. What was kept in it when your late master was alive?"

"Silver plate and sometimes money."

"Indeed. And who kept the key?"

"Mr. Mark kept it."

"The only one?"

"There was only one. Or so they said . . ."

"What do you mean, 'So they said'?"

"Well, Mr. Mark used to lock up his loose cash in the box. It's a bit of a stretch to the bank from here and he'd keep a few pounds handy about the house. He complained a time or two about notes bein' missin'. Once he said it looked as if somebody else could get in his box as well as himself. But he was that absent-minded—he very likely lost count of what he'd got, or else took the money himself and forgot. But you mentionin' it just reminded me of what he said."

The girl bent down to a large mirror standing on the floor

and by a feat of turning and twisting managed to see the reflection of her face in it, and pat her hair and adjust it to her satisfaction.

In the next room Hoar and Co. were busy again. There was a lot of scraping, clattering and banging and then somebody started to play the piano. It was not by any means an expert effort. The soloist picked out the tunes by ear and they were almost unrecognisable.

The girl flounced off to investigate, and Littlejohn was left alone.

There were sounds of arguing next door, and then a voice thundered out:

"Get out! You are no son of mine . . ."

Littlejohn, tired of waiting, went off to find the girl.

Sitting on a swivel piano-stool was the young man of the removers' party. His cigarette still dangled from his mouth. In front of him was a tall, white-haired, heavy man with a large nose, tinted by heavy drinking. It was Mr. William Hoar, denouncing his son for waywardness. By his side stood another old man, a better preserved replica of William. This was Mr. Ernest Hoar, proprietor of Hoar and Company. A long bi-forked white beard was suspended from his chin. He looked like Father Christmas. All had on green baize aprons and white jackets with H & Co. on the pockets.

"You are no son of mine . . ."

"Withdraw your curse, William," said Father Christmas in stern tones. "Or withdraw yourself from my employ."

William had once been a travelling actor, who, out of a job, had joined his brother in the removing business. He loved to dramatise everything. In the course of his touring he had begotten a son and become a widower at the same time. The son was also in the business, but, since a turn in the forces, had shown a disinclination to knuckle under to his parent, who spent his time in denouncing him as a result.

Littlejohn stood in the doorway taking in the crazy scene. The maid was flushed and angry-looking, as though the prodigal son had been trying to kiss or cuddle her. Which was exactly what had been happening when his father turned up . . .

"Did any of you have anything to do with the oak chest until recently owned by Mr. Curwen? I mean the one which recently figured in a murder case."

It was a shot in the dark. Littlejohn thought that as he was waiting he might as well make himself useful.

"And why should you want to know, sir? Sht, sht . . ."

Mr. William posed magnificently, as though defending the honour of his firm—or rather his brother's. He was so used to drinking, when he could get at it, that he made noises as though drawing in beer from a pint pot—sht, sht.

Father Christmas nodded approval. Hoar and Company were models of discretion and pledged to secrecy concerning clients' affairs, as their estimates stated. Estimates Free, by Road, Rail or Sea. Strictest Secrecy Maintained. Only Members of the Family Engaged in the Business.

Littlejohn explained the purpose of his visit. The Hoars gathered round like a flock of crows. William's nose glowed with enthusiasm and Ernest's hoary beard bristled and shone until it looked like a series of fine icicles stuck on his face. The younger generation of Hoar took out another fag, jammed it in the corner of its mouth, lit it, ogled the maid and set itself to listen if nothing else.

"What about a brew of tea, Lucy? I know we've not long 'ad one, but another wouldn't come amiss."

But the maid wasn't having any. She wasn't going to miss anything.

"What was the information you were seeking?" asked William, looking like Hamlet interrogating his father's ghost.

"I want to hear anything you might know about the box which was used in the recent murder. Men in your line of business sometimes have the handling of such goods. In particular, I'm trying to find out how many keys there were . . ."

"I've already told you," interrupted Lucy. "Only one. I should know."

"Quite right, my girl. You should know. But perhaps you don't. You see, there may have been a spare key with it when it came here."

Mr. Ernest Hoar spoke from somewhere in his beard. He sounded to be chewing some soft substance, so muffled was his voice.

"That box belonged to Mr. Curwen for fifteen years or more. I know, because I brought it here from The Towers, when Mr. Abraham Scorer was sold-up. I remember it well. We moved Mr. Scorer in and he went bankrupt before the bill was paid. We . . ."

"Was there one key, or two?"

Mr. William looked annoyed.

"Let my brother finish, sht, sht . . ."

Mr. Ernest nodded approval, which the brother supported by sht, sht, and again sht.

"I was going to say, there was only one key."

"You have a good memory, sir."

"I have. I remember taking the key from the lock, placing it in an envelope, making quite sure that there was not another, and handing it over to Mr. Curwen in the envelope when we delivered it."

"I see. Thank you."

Sht, sht, and another sht.

A key could be heard rattling in the lock of the front door and the house-removing party suddenly broke up and started vigorously to shift the chairs and tables. A lot of old scroungers, thought Littlejohn, as he went into the hall to see who was arriving.

In the inner doorway appeared a tall, well-built, handsome woman of forty or thereabouts. She was dark, with a good, ruddy complexion, a generous mouth, smouldering eyes, and black hair which shone like gunmetal as the light caught it. She raised her eyebrows at the sight of the visitor and raised them still more when she saw Lucy emerge from among the pantechnicon men.

"A gentleman from the police, Miss Barbara."

"Indeed. What do the police want with me? You can go, Lucy, and don't hinder the removal men."

"I was only . . ."

"That will do. I said you may go!"

No wonder the removers were hustling around! William and Ernest were busy with the piano.

"Take care with that, the pair of you. It's too heavy for only two. Now you, Harry, give the other two a hand."

"I just wanted a word with you, Miss Curwen, about the chest owned by your late father," said Littlejohn, impatient to be getting away from this bedlam. "You no doubt know that it is an exhibit in connection with the murder of Mr. Grossman?"

"Come into this room, Inspector. I'm sorry things are in such a mess. I'm due to be out of here to-day. You were saying . . . ?"

Littlejohn repeated his statement.

"Yes. I know it's a part of the case. But what has that to do with me? It was sold and taken away before that occurred."

She was very short about it and not at all pleased.

"Were there ever two keys to the box?"

"No. Only one. And my father always kept that in his pocket. Why?"

"The one key was in the possession of the buyer, who was miles away at the time of the crime. We're puzzled concerning how the body got in the box without the lock's being forced or something. And it was obviously unlocked, not forced."

"There was only one key."

"I see. And there was no other way? Say, a trick panel or something?"

"How absurd! No. It's been in the family for years, and the only way of opening it was with my father's key."

"Thank you, Miss Curwen. I think that's all I wanted to know. Did you ever have any dealings with Grossman and Small?"

"No. Never. They bought the box at an auction we held here not long ago. A sale of surplus furniture. Otherwise, I had nothing to do with them. Even then, the matter was settled through the auctioneer."

"I see. Did you know either Grossman or Small?"

"I just knew Mr. Grossman casually. I've met him a time or two at public functions and found him a very nice gentleman. I don't know Mr. Small at all."

"Was Mr. Grossman generally well-liked locally?"

Miss Curwen looked really annoyed.

"I'm sure I don't know, Inspector. Really, must we go on with this? As you can see, no doubt, I'm very busy."

Littlejohn wondered what all the annoyance was about. Surely the question was quite a civil one.

"I'm merely trying to find out as much about the dead man as possible. Mainly, had he any enemies? That is important."

"No doubt it is. But I can't give you the least information about him. Why should I be able to?"

Littlejohn detected a note of anxiety in her tone. He wondered why.

"In that case, I'll waste no more of your time, Miss Curwen. Good day, and thank you."

Outside, the piano was on the move. The three baize-aproned men were shuffling along and the strings of the instrument twanged and resounded as they shoved it here and there, lifting it, bumping it down, and again hoisting it over obstacles.

"Go easy . . ."

"Careful now . . . sht, sht, sht . . ."

"We'd do with another helper down these steps . . . sht, sht . . . Might I prevail upon you, sir, to give us a hand?"

"I'm no good at moving pianos," said Littlejohn, squeezing past and making rapidly for the gate.

He felt indignant at the nerve of the man, but when he turned and saw the trio trotting down the sloping path bearing aloft the instrument, the weight of which was hurling them onwards to what looked like certain disaster, he had to smile to himself.

He was not there to see the end of the incident.

## 8

### RIDGFIELD'S HOTEL

IN LONDON, Cromwell, Littlejohn's assistant, was busy at Ridgfield's Hotel. His chief had told him to get to know as much as possible about Mr. Grossman and what he did there.

The doorkeeper was huge, like a medieval headsman or torturer, and he had a harsh, steely glare for all intruders. He gave Cromwell a look of contempt. Ridgfield's was a very select hotel and their clients came year after year unto the third and fourth generation. A hushed, almost holy, atmosphere overhung the place, and elderly dowagers, bilious-looking colonial administrators, haughty fox-hunters of both sexes and a few of the milder scions of noble houses moved to and fro as though they owned the hotel, lock, stock and barrel.

The doorman thrust his greyhound's muzzle close to Cromwell's homely face.

"Sorry. Full up," he said, as though daring him to try to enter.

"Nobody asked you," replied Cromwell testily, and brandished his warrant card under the flunkey's nose. The man turned pale.

"Better see the hall porter . . ."

In his haste to be rid of him, the doorman spun Cromwell round the revolving door and passed him on to a colleague resplendent in gold braid and with a gimlet eye which seemed capable of giving you a blood-test to establish your status in the social order.

He looked disdainfully at Cromwell until the doorkeeper's whispered words suddenly changed his outlook.

"I'll tell the manager . . ."

The hall porter made off on flat feet to a small pen illuminated from within by a green-shaded light.

"Here, wait a minute. You'll do."

In the hall a man with a head like a pike, including teeth, and goggling eyes, one covered by a monocle, giving the impression that he had carried away a part of his aquarium, was analysing hole by hole his round of golf on the previous day.

"Usually take five on number one, but the blighter took four. So I . . ."

Cromwell felt he could handle the hall porter far better than the manager. He wanted no battles of wits with the proud, would-be emperor who ran the place.

"Come in 'ere, then."

The porter drew Cromwell into his quarters, which were little larger than a telephone kiosk and smelled strongly of surreptitious cigarettes and coke fumes, for it was over the flue.

You could still hear the pike bleating about his golf.

"On in three and a beauty of a putt waitin' for me . . ."

"Now, look snappy. I'm supposed to be on duty."

The porter seemed to be trying to do a hundred and one jobs at once. The window-cleaners were in and he kept watching them anxiously as though expecting them to fall at any minute. Judging from the alarm in his eyes, he might have been a spectator at a trapeze act in which the performers threatened at any moment to hurl hundreds of feet to their deaths.

"Do you know Mr. Grossman who used to come here from time to time?"

"Wot? The fellow that was murdered and stuffed in the oak box? Yes, knew 'im well. A regular client here."

"How often did he come?"

"Oh, about six times a year, and stayed anythin' from three days to a week at a time. Nice, gentlemanly chap. No trouble at all."

"Had he any friends here?"

The porter stroked his chin with a heavy, grating noise. He was a bulky man, out of condition through hanging about, doing little. His deputy, a strapping lad, new to the job, kept running in and out for instructions, as jumpy and nervous as an animal newly captive in a cage.

"Well? Had he any friends here?"

The corner of the porter's mouth lifted in a leer.

"Well . . . I never seen him with anybody. But strictly on the q.t., one of the chambermaids told me he had a lady friend. She used to stay 'ere as well. Come a day or so before 'im, and left a day or so after."

The man had relaxed into easy colloquial talk, free from many aspirates. Like a linguist who switches from one language to another as occasion demands. Before the haughty clients he spoke with heavy, laboured correctness.

"Go on with you!"

Cromwell knew the best way to get a full tale was to challenge the man's statement.

"It's true, I tell yer. I know the woman, although I didn't associate the two of 'em till the maid mentioned it. She found dark hairs in the little chap's bedroom. And 'im with hair like silver. I ask you . . ."

"What was the woman called?"

"Now I ain't going to give anything away. Much as my job's worth."

A small procession passed the door. The head-waiter preparing for a meal. He had cruel, green eyes which looked right through the smaller mortals in his path. He was followed by a tall, willowy, swarthy underling with a small black moustache and greasy, undulating hair, wheeling a trolley of *hors d'œuvres,* each dish looking like a variation on the same theme, a species of seaweed.

"You're going to talk right now, unless you want to let yourself in for a peck of trouble. I'm not leaving without the information," said Cromwell in his best official tones. He thrust his craggy jaw close to that of the lackey, who burst into a cold sweat as he wrestled with his problems.

"I'll 'ave to speak to the management . . ."

"You'll do nothing of the sort. You've handled the woman's baggage and know where she came from. Now come on. I've not got all day."

The golfer's voice still rang round the place:

"At number five I drove with my iron . . ."

Had his small son discussed his games of marbles with half the ferocity and detail, he would have been smacked and put to bed.

"Who was she, and where did she come from?"

"She came from Fetling, same as Mr. Grossman."

"What was her name?"

"Smith . . ."

"Go on! You don't expect me to fall for that."

"It's true. S'welp me, it is."

"Didn't you check identity cards as visitors registered?"

The flunkey raised his eyebrows in horror. They were long and straggling, like the antennae of a strange insect.

"Wot! 'ere? Good Lord, no! As much as our reputation's worth. We *know* all our clients. Come year after year, they do. Smith it was, before ever identity cards came out."

"Well, well. What was she like?"

"Tall. Smartly turned-out. Haughty piece o' work, too."

"A very illuminating description."

"Gimme a chance. Well-built—nice, oval face—and hair . . . Lemme see . . . ?"

The porter raised his eyes and eyebrows heavenwards as though praying the gods for inspiration, and again grated his chin.

". . . Hair . . . raven black, as you might say, with a sort of blue sheen when the light caught it. Good complexion. That's about all."

"Very helpful—very helpful indeed. Probably hundreds like her walking down the Haymarket at this very minute."

"Well, I've done my best."

"You don't mean to tell me that she registered here under a false name and got away with it?"

"It mightn't have been false. People *are* called Smith. Lots of 'em. They . . ."

"Oh, yes, yes, yes. Bags of 'em. But this one sounds fishy to me. Is the chambermaid still here?"

"Yes. But . . ."

"No buts. Get her."

Cromwell was fed-up with trying to squeeze blood out of a stone.

"Hi!"

The gold-braided majordomo called a passing page-boy.

"Go up the back stairs and bring Martha down off the second floor. Tell her to come here to me."

"O.K."

"And don't say 'O.K.' to me. Get a move on."

"O.K."

Outside, the pike had reached the tenth hole.

"A sitter . . . and I missed the damn' thing by a whisker . . ."

"Oh, damn' bad luck, ole man . . ."

Martha, the chambermaid, was a dumpy, middle-aged, bothered-looking girl, with grey, wispy hair and a patient, faithful air of resignation.

"Martha, this is a man from Scotland Yard. Wants to ask you a question or two. Confidential, it is, and not to be repeated out of this 'ere room . . ."

"I wouldn't think of it, Mr. Haythornthwaite."

So that was the name of the braided pundit. Well, well. Too nice a name by far.

The maid stood humbly before Cromwell, her fingers pleating her apron, her cap a little awry, her cheeks flushed with excitement.

"Tell her who we're talking about."

"The Sergeant's asking about Mr. Grossman's lady friend. You know the one, Martha, Miss Smith."

"Oh, yes."

The girl blushed at the thought of goings-on under her very eye. Experience in hotel bedrooms did not seem to have given her any veneer of sophistication.

"*Was* her name Smith?" asked Cromwell.

"That's what she registered as."

"I know all about that. But did you come across any evidence that she had another name?"

"I don't think that was 'er name, sir, but she was that careful. Never left anything about with her real name on. Locked 'er bags and 'er dressing-case and never left any letters or nothin' lyin' about. Even her hair brushes and things that might 'ave had initials on was locked away."

"I see. And that was why you thought her name wasn't Smith. But that might have been ordinary precaution. Some people are that way, you know."

"Yes. But she forgot one thing. She left a handkerchief under her pillow one time with initials on. The initial wasn't Smith . . . I mean, not an S."

"What was it?"

Martha hesitated.

Cromwell guessed what had happened.

"Right, you can get back to your job," he said to the hall-porter. Probably the girl would talk better without him.

The flunkey looked glad to get away, and made a hasty exit. He could be heard making up for lost time by ordering around the page-boys and window-cleaners who, in his absence, had been gossiping in mid-air from the tops of their ladders.

"At number thirteen I muffed my drive. Bloody awful stroke. Must have taken my eye off the ball. Dunno . . ."

"You can't be too careful, ole man. Even the best of us . . ."

"Now, Martha, did you keep the handkerchief?"

The girl looked ready to weep. Already she saw herself in a prison cell.

"I—I—She was goin' away that day, and I forgot . . ."

"Don't worry. I'm not blaming you. I guess those sort of things come to you as perquisites. All I want to know is, what were the initials? Come along. This is wasting my time."

"I 'ave the handky in my room. It was such a good one, I kept it for one of me best. Thought when I'd time I'd take off the initials and put on me own. But I don't seem to get the time."

"Bring it here, then."

Relieved, the girl scuttered away, and soon was back with the piece of embroidered lawn.

"Here it is."

The initials were *B.C.*

"Thank you, Martha. Sorry. I'll have to take this. But here's half-a-crown to buy yourself another. Sorry I can't give you any coupons!"

"That's all right, sir. I didn't want anything."

The girl was almost crying with relief.

"And you won't tell Mr. Haythornthwaite about the handky—they're most particular here. Much as my job's worth . . ."

"Don't worry, Martha, I won't. Thank you. That's all."

It was lunch time. The guests were making their way to food, like members of a religious procession, hesitating at the door of the dining-room, anxious to show that they were too polite to be eager to be getting at the eatables. The head-waiter was bowing them in, like a burgomaster surrendering his city to the conquerors. The hall-porter, too, was civilly trying to catch the eye and greet those who tipped well when they left.

"O.K.?" he managed to say to Cromwell out of the corner of his mouth.

"O.K." answered Cromwell, and remembering the reprimanded page-boy, grinned to the discomfiture of the gold braid.

The golfing pike was not going to eat until he had finished his round.

"At the seventeenth, I got a lovely one . . ."

His mandibles snapped and he rolled his protruding eyes in ecstasy. His companion looked anxiously at the dining-room door.

The doorman spun the revolving door for Cromwell and even saluted . . .

Cromwell was disappointed with his efforts. He had hoped to wring a tale of intrigue, jealousy, threats and even a scuffle or two out of the hotel staff. Instead, he'd got a tale of an almost comic, furtive little affair, probably of no consequence whatever.

But when he telephoned the results to Littlejohn, the Inspector could not restrain a shout of enthusiasm, which brought to Cromwell's mournful face the wintry smile which always shows he is pleased with himself.

So, leaving the telephone, he went and stood himself a drink.

## 9

### THE SECOND KEY

LITTLEJOHN turned in at the police-station for an early word with Superintendent Gillespie, whom he found engaged. The sergeant in the charge-room, however, told Littlejohn to walk right in, as Gillespie was anxious to see him.

Gillespie was wearing his hat, from which Littlejohn judged that his gall-bladder, or whatever it was which accounted for his strange moods, had turned upon the Fetling man again.

"Come in, Inspector," said Gillespie, without so much as a good-morning. "These people really want to see *you*."

He said it with great asperity, as though he thought Littlejohn ought to have been there earlier to relieve him of an unpleasant interview.

The visitors consisted of a small, militant woman, and a huge, meek man.

"This is Mrs. Hollis . . ."

The little woman cast a malevolent glance at Littlejohn, who wondered what he'd done wrong. She was dressed in her best Sunday-go-to-meeting clothes; a black costume with a skirt too long, a black blouse with the photograph of a lad in R.A.F. uniform in a brooch pinned on her breast, and a hideous black hat which fitted like a misshaped bell over her ears.

"I brought Mr. 'ollis with me. He'll see that I'm treated proper . . ."

"Yuss," rumbled Mr. 'ollis.

He, too, was dressed in his best black, carried a bowler hat shaped like a melon, wore large, squeaking boots, and stood like a criminal expecting a long sentence. He had a fresh, ruddy face, a large, dark moustache, bristly hair with a calf-lick drooping over his narrow forehead, and sad, brown eyes, like those of a spaniel, in loose sockets.

"Yuss," said Mr. Hollis, and cleared his throat the better to articulate. Then he seemed to forget what he had to say and closed his mouth again.

"I'll leave 'em to you," said Gillespie biliously, and with a brief nod, rose, left the room and started to chase around his subordinates.

Littlejohn sat down in the vacant chair.

"Now, Mrs. Hollis, what can I do for you?"

Mrs. Hollis rose like a furious bantam cock.

"Miss Adlestrop, who I saw last night when I got 'ome, told me the police was comin' to see me to-morrer. That was last night. To-morrer now meaning to-day . . ."

She gave a twitch of her head to show that she knew all about it.

"Yuss," endorsed Mr. Hollis.

"Well?"

"Well, I don't want no police hangin' round my house. I've allus been respectable and well thought of, paying me way and doin' me duty accordin' to me lights, and I don't want me good name in the village spoilin' by police being seen callin' at my place . . ."

She came up for air and took a huge gulp.

Mr. Hollis thumped the table limply with a huge fist as though to confirm forcibly what his good woman was saying, but did not speak.

"But, my dear Mrs. Hollis, nobody would have known it was the police. I was going to call on you myself to ask a question or two about what happened on the day the body of Mr. Grossman turned up at Miss Adlestrop's . . . That's all."

"And quite enough, I says. And don't you think as all the village doesn't know who you are, with Mister Councillor Blanket talkin' all over the place about him helpin' you to solve the crime. Don't you think you ain't known, because you are. All the village'll be at their doors next time you call, just to have a good look. An' I'm not havin' 'em seein' you enterin' my place. They'll think I'm mixed up in this murder, which I'm not."

"Yuss," intoned Mr. 'ollis, and then realising that he was wrong he changed it to "No."

Littlejohn decided he'd had quite enough of arguing the point, so changed his tack.

"Well, and now that you're here, we might as well have a little talk, Mrs. Hollis."

"That's what I come for. Here's the place for police business, not the 'omes of respectable, hard-workin' people."

"Yuss," emphatically stated Mr. Hollis. He was very respectable, but not hard-working. He was described as a jobbing-gardener at the Labour Exchange, but most of his jobbing consisted in dodging the gardening. He contrived to make a rather satisfactory living out of mowing the lawns of local residents who possessed petrol-driven mowers. When the back-bending work was suggested, he was always called away to another client on his rota, or else to the 'local' which bore the ambiguous name of *The Wanderer's Home*.

"Yuss," said Mr. Hollis, and again "Yuss."

"Well then, I hear that you cleaned the oak chest after P.C. Puddiphatt had removed the body . . ."

"I did. And it needed it if it was to stop in that house,

which it didn't, Miss Adlestrop 'avin kindly given it to me not bein' able to bear it after wot was in it, and me bein' used to that sort o' thing, havin' laid out corpses for thirty years and more . . ."

"Yuss," said Mr. Hollis, with great admiration and satisfaction.

"You cleaned out the box. Now, Mrs. Hollis, was there anything in the box after Mr. Grossman's body was removed?"

"No. Only dust as them lazy ones at the *Whistler's Rest,* or whatever they call their silly place, had left in it. Some people's born dirty. Once dirty, always dirty, I sez . . ."

Mr. Hollis nodded his calf-lick profoundly.

"Yuss," he groaned.

"Are you sure there was nothing else, Mrs. Hollis? Think carefully."

Mrs. Hollis seemed to ponder deeply and so did her husband.

"No . . ."

"Not a little flag from the Fetling Children's flag-day?"

"Why . . . yes . . ."

"Yuss," shouted Mr. Hollis with gusto and looked delighted with his wife's feat of recollection. He even rose and took a pace or two about the room, preening himself.

"The flag was in the box when you started to clean it up?"

"No. It fell on the floor as Puddiphatt lifted the body out. You know, I went an' forgot all about it from that day to this . . ."

Mr. Hollis sat down and looked heartbroken at his wife's lapse of memory.

"You're sure it was with the body in the box?"

"I've said so, haven't I? When I say a thing I mean it."

Her husband raised himself and looked round as though

ready to take on anybody who dared to doubt his wife's veracity.

"Very well, Mrs. Hollis. Thank you for calling."

"I called because I 'ad to. I won't 'ave no police round my place makin' people talk . . ."

"And you've nothing else to say which might interest us? Anything unusual about the body or the behaviour of anyone present?"

"No. A pore little body, if you ask me," said Mrs. Hollis with the wisdom of an expert layer-out. "And as fer the behaviour of those present. Disgustin' I calls it. Faintin' and throwin' fits all over the place at the sight of one little corp. Where would folks be if everybody did that . . .?"

She looked challengingly at Littlejohn. "Yuss," said Mr. Hollis with great indignation.

"Where would everybody be? A dead body's a dead body and faintin' and hystericking all over the place won't make it any other . . . But I slapped their faces for 'em, I did that."

She smacked her thin lips with satisfaction and Mr. Hollis joined her in making clicking noises against the vulcanite plate which held his false teeth.

Mrs. Hollis rose, pulled on her string gloves, took up her umbrella and gave her black hat a twitch.

"Come on, Lambert," she said. And then, turning belligerently on Littlejohn, "And don't you come callin' at my place, see? I took the trouble to come all this way and I don't want any journey in vain or any of my good name spoilin'."

"Thank you for the journey, both of you. I'll see that you're not troubled."

"See you don't," said Mr. Hollis with a vigorous and threatening nod of the head. And as though surprised to find that he had more words than bare affirmative and negative in his vocabulary, he repeated them. "See you don't . . ."

He looked ready to say it a third time, when Gillespie entered. He had on his face a feline expression, that of a cantankerous cat which sees a dog.

"And next time you're mixed up with a murdered body, Mrs. Hollis, don't wipe out all the fingerprints," he said, apparently unable to let bygones be bygones.

"Well . . . I like that! After me comin' all the way to Fetling and leavin' me work . . ."

The mention of leaving work seemed to stimulate Mr. Hollis. After all, he didn't earn enough with his jobbing to keep them both, and his wife made up the bulk of the budget by 'obliging'.

"Hey!" he said, his voice becoming shrill with emotion. He prodded Gillespie's tunic with a large, dirty-nailed index. "Hey! Don't you insult my missus . . ."

Again surprised at his new access of words, he paused and repeated himself.

"Don't you insult my missus, see?"

"Come on, Lambert. We don't want no bother. You can see he's no gentleman . . ."

And with this parting shot, Mrs. Hollis drew her partner from the room, but not before Mr. 'ollis had delivered his final threat.

"Don't you insult my missus, see . . . ?"

They heard him say it for a fourth time to the man in the charge-room and presumably he uttered it all the way home.

Left to himself, Gillespie thawed to the extent of telling Littlejohn he didn't feel so well that morning.

"I'm sorry to hear that . . . What's the matter?"

"Liverish . . . Had some fish and chips for supper and they laid heavily on me all night . . ."

Littlejohn almost told him he ought to have had more sense with a liver and gall-bladder like his, but thought the time hardly suitable.

Outside a barrel organ was playing:

> Am I wasting my time,
> By thinking you're mine,
> And dreaming the way that I do . . .

"Oh, for God's sake," yelled the liverish Superintendent. "Groves! Groves!! Clear that damn' musical merchant off or I'll go mad . . ."

When he'd calmed down, Littlejohn told Gillespie about the flag found with Grossman's body.

"Children's Home, eh? H'm. I'll have a word with Miss Sharpes, the secretary, about it. She'll know who was selling them. Maybe, we could find out where, between *The Seven Whistlers* and the station, or even Hartsbury, that flag was sold."

"Bit of a job. When was the flag-day?"

Gillespie rang the bell at his elbow.

"Groves! Just look up the file and find out when the Children's Home flag-day was."

"Last Tuesday, sir."

"I said look it up! Want it in black and white."

Groves made a crestfallen exit and returned with written confirmation of his statement.

"Last Tuesday," said Gillespie with a measure of pride, as though he'd found it all out himself.

"But Grossman was killed on Monday. How come the flag to be there? Were they selling them the day before?"

"Certainly not! We give permission for flag-days here and one day doesn't mean two. Now, that's very interesting. I'd like to know who had the nerve to start selling flags the day before."

It might not have been a murder case at all!

"That's what we ought to find out from your Miss Sharpes, Gillespie."

"You bet we will!" replied Gillespie with relish.

"Then I'll leave you to do it," said Littlejohn, and made off.

"Groves! Groves!! Send in Robinshaw," yelled Gillespie.

But Groves was in the street arguing with a wandering minstrel who was defending his rights. He was playing gramophone records on a portable instrument, and sitting on the pavement was a small, sad-looking dog clad in a coat with mother-of-pearl buttons and with an alms-cup tied round its neck.

> Am I wasting my time,
> By thinking you're mine . . .

Barbara Curwen made a gesture of impatience when Littlejohn again called at her house. She was distant and haughty, but her front soon caved-in when the Inspector came straight to the point.

"Why didn't you tell me you were a friend of Mr. Grossman, Miss Curwen?" he asked.

All the blood drained from her face, throwing into vivid relief the scarlet gash of her lips.

"What do you mean?"

But her expression had already answered Littlejohn's question.

"You were frequently seen with Mr. Grossman at Ridgfield's Hotel in London, Miss Curwen."

"I have nothing to say."

"Very well. In that case you'll be called at the adjourned inquest to answer under oath. Good day."

Littlejohn made for the door.

In the passage Messrs. Hoar were still moving things about. This time it was a harmonium.

"Stop!!"

Barbara Curwen decided to talk. Hesitant, nervous, her self-control stretched to breaking-point, she told Littlejohn of her friendship with Grossman. Of course, she didn't admit to being his mistress. She skirted that point and Littlejohn did not press it at the time. Both had stayed at Ridgfield's and, coming from the same town, had naturally struck up a friendship. They had gone to shows together—and so on.

"And were you still on good terms with Mr. Grossman when he died?"

Miss Curwen's eyes flickered.

"Yes."

Littlejohn didn't believe her.

"Where were you when he was killed, Miss Curwen?"

"In London . . ."

"Ridgfield's?"

"Yes."

"What were you doing between eight and nine on the night of the crime?"

She looked astonished.

"Surely . . . I was at the theatre."

"Which, please?"

*"The Embankment."*

"What did you see?"

" *'I've Just Killed Stracey.'* "

That was right. Littlejohn had taken Letty to see the show on his birthday. He liked to see a good crime play by way of relaxation.

"Anybody with you or did anyone see you there?"

"No, I went alone. But the porter at the hotel saw me come in about eleven. I couldn't possibly have got back to Fetling, killed Mr. Grossman, and then returned to Ridgfield's in the time, if that's what you're getting at, Inspector. I think you're being a little absurd."

"That's for me to judge. And now, about the box. You're sure there was only one key?"

Her expression gave her away again!

"So there *were* two keys, after all. Why didn't you tell me the truth when I called before, Miss Curwen? You've wasted a lot of my time."

She was like a schoolgirl caught in a guilty act. She flushed scarlet and then, pulling herself together, met Littlejohn's calm look with defiance.

"If you want to know, I had a key made for myself. My father was extremely mean with housekeeping money and my allowance. He kept cash in the box . . . Once, when he left the key in by mistake, I took it, had impressions made and had a new key cut for myself, so that in emergencies I could get money. I never told anyone . . . I was too ashamed . . ."

"And what happened to the key after you sold the box?"

"I gave it to Mr. Grossman and asked him to say nothing about it. I didn't want the servants to know . . . Father had complained in his lifetime about missing money and I'd always told him not to be silly, there was only one key . . ."

"Funny you took all the trouble to give the second key to Mr. Grossman when you could have thrown it away."

"I happened to meet him and the box was mentioned. I'd given him my key before I'd quite realised the implications."

"But why didn't you tell me that when I called before?"

"I thought you'd question me and suspect that I'd had a hand in the murder and that my relations with Mr. Grossman would all come out and cause a scandal. I didn't kill him . . . I swear I didn't . . ."

She looked on the verge of collapse.

"What about these packing cases, madam? We've got to

finish by late afternoon, you see, as you've to give up the key to-day . . ."

It was Father Christmas Hoar anxious to be getting on with the job and finished before the pubs opened. He relieved the situation, and Littlejohn departed, leaving him in possession.

' 10 '

THE SEVEN WHISTLERS AGAIN

A PRETTY kettle of fish! Two keys now! Well, there wasn't a key in Grossman's pocket or possessions, which the police had overhauled with great vigour and thoroughness.

So somebody had taken one key.

After telephoning to Cromwell to see the porter at Ridgfields again and check Barbara Curwen's alibi, such as it was, Littlejohn returned to the antique shop.

Before he left, however, Gillespie dropped a bombshell!

"My wife says she'd like to meet you," he said, like one passing on orders from a superior officer. "So, if you care to come round to tea this afternoon . . . We might talk things over over a pipe after . . ."

A note of apology crept into Gillespie's tones.

"It'll be a pleasure," said Littlejohn. "You can show me your pigeons, too . . ."

Gillespie's expression changed with great suddenness. It was as though somebody had given him a powerful dose of medicine and washed the bile from his system.

"Yes . . . Yes . . . By jove! And, by the way, I've put Robinshaw on hunting round and about who sold flags a day before the event. He'll probably be along with his report in the course of the evening. He's engaged to my daughter . . ."

Well, well. So Gillespie had a daughter . . . And loved by

a policeman, too. Littlejohn found himself half hoping, for Robinshaw's sake, that she took after her mother. He changed his mind later. Meanwhile he arranged to call at the police station in time to be led to tea by Gillespie and made his way to *The Seven Whistlers* again.

Mrs. Doakes was nowhere to be seen. Small, however, was in the shop arguing about the price of a Welsh dresser with a large, masculine woman who seemed to be trying to beat him down by sheer avoirdupois. Unsuccessful, she stamped out, rattling all the glass and china and slamming the door.

"Whew . . ! That's Mrs. Gillespie . . . A proper tartar."

Littlejohn felt his heart sink.

"What is it now?"

Small looked anything but pleased, and flopping down in a chair, took out a soft packet of small cigarettes and inserted one in his huge and ugly face. His eyes drew together in a fearful squint as he applied a match and made him more forbidding than ever.

"Did you know there were two keys to Curwen's box, Mr. Small?"

The fat man paused, holding the lighted match half-way back from his mouth, extinguished it by shaking it in the air and then flung it on the floor.

"No. There weren't two . . ."

"Yes, there were."

"Who told yer . . . ?"

He drew in a huge gulp of smoke, coughed, cleared his throat and spat revoltingly in the fire.

"Miss Curwen. Was there a key in the lock when you got it here?"

"I told yer, I washed my hands of it when I heard what Grossman had paid for it. I don't know a thing about it . . ."

"Who packed it for the train?"

"My niece, Mrs. Doakes . . ."

"Is she in?"

"No. She's gone to a sale up-town."

"She stitched up the canvas covering in which it was sent to Hartsbury, as well?"

"Yes. She always does that sort of job. Why?"

"I'll call again. I'd like another word with her."

"Sale won't be over till tea-time . . ."

Tea-time! Littlejohn thought with a sense of foreboding of tea with the formidable Mrs. Gillespie and her liverish husband.

"I'll call again . . ."

They sat down to high-tea at the Gillespie's at half-past six. There were the local Superintendent, his wife, their daughter Ethel, young Gillespie, just finishing at the grammar school and with pimples all over his face, and Littlejohn. There was also a vacant place, laid and ready for the absent Robinshaw.

They were eating fresh salmon.

"Difficult to get these days . . . Help yourself, Inspector Littlejohn," boomed Mrs. Gillespie. "Seven and sixpence a pound!"

That was the trouble with Mrs. Gillespie. She had come into money and they weren't dependent on the Superintendent's earnings. She liked that to be known.

Gillespie looked at the salmon as though he wished it would choke him and put him out of his misery. Ethel blushed and glanced sideways and reproachfully at her enormous mother, and young Gillespie didn't seem to hear, for he was all eyes for Littlejohn, and Scotland Yard was a magic word to his ears.

Mrs. Gillespie finished serving the tea, lifted her bosom on the table and started to tuck in. She had a long, heavy face, three chins, a tapering, mischievous nose and small, brown busy eyes. As she ministered to her brood the many rings flashed on her fingers.

"Show the Inspector the watch your grandad gave you when you passed Matric., Denzil," she said, smacking her lips over the salmon and cucumber. "Cost forty pounds . . . His grandad—my father—was that pleased with Denzil coming through."

Denzil didn't seem to hear. He kept smiling at Littlejohn and his pimples shone with eager reverence.

"Denzil!!"

The poor lad produced the watch without much enthusiasm. It was a large hunter with a ponderous albert attached. Denzil had asked for a wrist-watch, like the rest of them wore. But no, Grandad Partington had no room for half measures. When he bought a watch, he bought a watch. Chain and all! Denzil concealed the chain in his pocket instead of displaying it across his waistcoat, and, hence, moved about with a large protuberance like a malignant growth across his abdomen.

"Very nice," said Littlejohn. "Thanks, Denzil."

It was nice to be called Denzil by a Scotland Yard detective. Something to tell the chaps to-morrow. Denzil glowed all over. He never saw much distinction in his own father. The terror of malefactors in Fetling was very quiet at home. So far, he'd hardly spoken a word.

"Gilbert's late!"

Mrs. Gillespie looked at the plate in front of the vacant chair as though about to demolish poor Robinshaw's tea as well as her own if he didn't turn-up soon.

"Duty comes first," ventured Gillespie. "He's a fair bit to do to-day."

"Well, you shouldn't have invited him to his tea then if he can't be here in time. . . ."

"Mother!!" said Ethel.

Littlejohn wondered whom Ethel took after. She certainly didn't strongly resemble either parent, yet, but there was a framed photograph on the wall of what looked like a deflated Mrs. Gillespie at about twenty-four or five which gave Littlejohn the thought that Robinshaw was in for a similar fate to that of his superior officer in, say, twenty years' time. As Littlejohn cautiously studied Ethel over his salmon and greens, he marvelled at nature and natural selection. You could see Mr. and Mrs. Gillespie subtly blended in that face. No distinct likeness, but as though nature had vigorously shaken up the bottle to make an equal mixture without displaying the individual ingredients.

And as for natural selection . . . He wondered what Robinshaw saw. . . .

Heavy feet plodded up the front garden path, paused, shuffled on the doorstep as the newcomer vigorously wiped his soles, and then the bell rang. Ethel excused herself, leapt up like a wild animal after its prey, they could hear her bossing Robinshaw about in the lobby, and then she led him in like an ox to slaughter.

Robinshaw was a huge ox. Round, red face; round, red hands; round, red nose; and a round, red head. His body was well padded and round, too, and probably under his clothes was red as well from embarrassment, for he was blushing as he entered. He was overcome when he saw Littlejohn. This was the last straw! He almost kowtowed with awe.

"Sit down and help yourself, Gilbert," said Mrs. Gillespie, passing the bread and butter to her future son-in-law before he had properly seated himself. "Fresh salmon, Gilbert. . . ."

Gilbert smiled back sheepishly at her. Littlejohn got the impression that Gilbert was a great favourite with Mrs. Gillespie, for she began to ladle extra salmon and cucumber on his plate before he had started, just to show he was specially favoured.

"Well?" asked Gillespie, portentously. "Any luck with the flag-day?"

"Yes," said Robinshaw, through a mouthful of food. In fact his mouth was overflowing with food, as though he might be trying to convey to his hostess that it was so good that he couldn't get it down fast enough. "Yes. . . ."

"Wait till after. No business over meals."

Mrs. Gillespie put her foot down and there was another awkward silence.

Robinshaw ogled Ethel. In spite of what you might think when you saw Mrs. Gillespie mothering him, Gilbert had really fallen in love at first sight with Ethel. Why, nature and her methods of selection alone could say.

It had been quite a romance. Ethel was secretary to the managing director of a large stores and had a nice and peaceful job with a very considerate boss. Then somebody had started, every morning at ten, ringing her up on the telephone, saying: "Miss Gillespie? I love you, Miss Gillespie," and hanging up. The thing had got on her nerves. Not only because of the monotony of it, day in and day out at the same time, but it is appalling to have a lover on your track and not know who it is.

So, at her wits' end, Ethel had spoken to father, who had put a detective on the job. And that detective was Gilbert Robinshaw. They had never been able to trace the phantom lover, who, apparently, hearing that the local sleuths were after him, had controlled his passion and sheered off. But it brought Gilbert and Ethel into contact and cooked Robinshaw's matrimonial goose for him. Father, spurred on by mother, had asked Robinshaw his intentions before he'd even kissed the girl!

Whenever Gilbert Robinshaw passed a telephone kiosk,

there came to him an overpowering desire to enter it, cover the mouthpiece with his handkerchief to muffle his voice, dial Fetling 4321: "Hankey's Stores? That you, Miss Gillespie? I love you. . . ." Then he would burst into a cold sweat.

"Shall we go into the front room while the women clear away?"

Gillespie rose with a sigh.

Robinshaw was meticulously clearing his plate of the last of some trifle. Bit by bit with a spoon, like a cat licking up the last drop.

"There's a fire in *the lounge*."

Gillespie would keep calling the lounge "the front room" and his wife objected to it. Since she came into Uncle Joe's money, made out of mineral waters, she'd set about social climbing. She hadn't met with phenomenal success and put it down to Gillespie's lack of co-operation.

The front room was full of new furniture, with a thick carpet on the floor. Vaguely, Littlejohn thought of hire-purchase. It was the sort of stuff you paid for by instalments. Had Mrs. Gillespie been able to read his thoughts, he'd have been shown the door. . . .

"Have a drink?"

Gillespie opened an enormous cocktail cabinet full of every kind of available drink, with a large display of glasses, bottles and the usual tackle for mixing and taking alcohol. It was Mrs. Gillespie's present to him last Christmas. He looked sheepish as he handled it, like a humble man who's been given a luxury car he can't get comfortable in or keep up.

"I'll have a bottle of beer, if I may. . . ."

Gillespie's face lit up. He was relieved and went off into the interior of the house for the beer. Outside, you could hear Mrs. Gillespie grumbling at him in stage whispers for not pressing more arrogant drinks on their distinguished guest.

Robinshaw had visited the secretary of the flag fund and had caused a bit of commotion, for she knew of Gillespie's strictness about flag-day regulations and saw herself hauled before the magistrates for misdemeanour. She herself had not touted in the street, of course. Too busy for that. Counting the money and telling others what to do. She'd given emphatic instructions that the sellers must not start until the authorised morning. Who had disobeyed? Breathing fire and fury, she had shown Robinshaw the list of saleswomen. There were thirty-four of them! Poor Gilbert had almost fainted at the thought of so much tramping up and down the town.

"I wouldn't be surprised if it wasn't that Mrs. Cleethorpes," said Mrs. Featherfew, the secretary. "A most wilful and disobedient woman. Although I must say her collections are always near the top of the list."

Littlejohn puffed his pipe and drank his beer calmly. It was good beer, the room was warm, and the instalment-like easy-chair at least comfortable. He could picture Mrs. Cleethorpes. In a hurry to be rid of her flags and get her box full. Brushing aside the secretary's regulations as fussy, and getting on the job at once.

"So I called to see Mrs. Cleethorpes first. . . ."

Robinshaw was slow and ponderous, and consulted his notebook from time to time, just to make it appear official. He had asked his prospective father-in-law for a whisky and soda, because he could get beer anywhere. He grew in importance as the drink began to take hold of him. He also grew a little amorous and speeded up his narrative in the hope that Littlejohn would get it over and be off and leave him and Ethel for half an hour's canoodling on their own in the front room before Gilbert said good-night.

". . . She owned up right away."

"What sort of a woman was she?"

"Eh?"

"What sort of a woman was she?"

"Little, and stout. Sort of always on the move. Bit uppish and defiant, like . . ."

Littlejohn could imagine her. He knew the sort. Bossy and knowing better than anybody else what they ought to do and how to do it. Probably brought up a large family and done well for them. . . .

"She said she'd almost sold all her flags on the night before the authorised day. And if we wanted to do anything about it, we could take her to court and she'd ask the magistrates what they thought they were doing wasting the time of honest people who worked for charity free of charge . . ."

"Where was her pitch?"

"Pitch? Oh yes . . . She'd the street just off the promenade. Water Avenue, it's called. A busy street—one of the main thoroughfares to the sea front. *The Palace* is there, too. She sold a lot to people going to the pictures. There are two entrances to *The Palace*; one in the Avenue for the cheap seats and one on the Prom. for the better ones. She seems to have been busy between the two doors."

"*The Palace,* eh?"

That was where Mrs. Doakes had been on the night of the crime. But wait . . .

"Where is the Bay Hotel?"

"Same place. *Palace* is at one corner of the Avenue; Bay Hotel's at the other. Why?"

So Small might have bought a flag, as well. In fact, so many flags were sold that half the town might have bought them.

Robinshaw looked cunningly at Littlejohn.

"I asked Mrs. Cleethorpes if she remembered selling flags to Mr. Small and Mrs. Doakes. . . ."

A very self-satisfied smile. He turned it on Gillespie, too. A sort of congratulation on securing such a smart son-in-law-to-be.

"Good! What did she say?"

Robinshaw kept up the dramatic suspense by taking another swig of his whisky and soda. Then he gazed invitingly at his empty glass, but Gillespie didn't bite. He looked ready to have another bilious attack. . . .

"She said she remembered selling one to Small as he went in the Bay Hotel. I asked her the time. She knew that, too. Quarter to eight. She remembered because the picture people had all gone in and there wasn't much of a queue for the second house. So things being a bit slack, she almost followed Small into the hotel for a cup of coffee."

"Good! What about the woman—Mrs. Doakes?"

"She doesn't remember her at all. When Mrs. Cleethorpes got to Water Avenue after collecting her flags and box, she found long queues at both doors of the picture house and went along the length of them. She was so busy taking money and handing out flags she hadn't time to look at everybody's face. She didn't remember seeing Mrs. Doakes, though she might easily have sold her a flag. . . ."

"H'm. All the same, that's good work, Robinshaw. Very helpful."

Gilbert leaned back in his chair and looked very pleased with himself. He wished Ethel had been there to hear Littlejohn praising him. He'd have something to tell her when he got her to himself. Stimulated by his success and the whisky inside him, he rose, walked solemnly to the cabinet and calmly helped himself to another liberal drink.

Gillespie, who was about to add his congratulations to those of Littlejohn, bit them back and glared at Robinshaw, who gave him a friendly nod. A credit to his father-in-law-to-be's force! Eh?

"Any ideas on the subject?" asked Gillespie, pouring out another beer for Littlejohn.

"Not much. . . . It's a question of motive, first, and so far we haven't unearthed a thing. We've an idea of how Grossman was killed, but *why,* that's another matter. We'll just have to keep on digging away till we turn up something. Barbara Curwen seems to have been Grossman's mistress."

Robinshaw's jaw fell, and he blushed furiously. Things like that weren't talked about where he came from, except in whispers. The impact of the words bowled him over and he took a good drink to brace himself. Then he grinned.

"She's an alibi of sorts, which I'm having checked."

"H'm. The Chief Constable'll be after my blood if we don't find something out soon. . . ."

Gillespie looked very cast down. He took a good drink to drown his sorrow.

Littlejohn looked at his watch. Eight-thirty.

"I think, if you'll excuse me, I'll be getting along. I want a word with the doorkeeper of *The Palace* before he goes."

Ethel and Mrs. Gillespie had entered. The elder woman looked at the cocktail cabinet and then at the beers of Littlejohn and her husband.

"Won't you have a better drink than that?" she said, indicating red, green, amber and colourless fluids.

"No thanks. I'm just off, Mrs. Gillespie. I've still some work to do. . . ."

"Not going already?"

Ethel was exchanging secret glances with her lover, who returned them with alcoholic fervour.

Young Gillespie arrived with an autograph album and begged Littlejohn's signature, greatly to the disgust of his father, who had never been asked for his.

Gillespie and his wife saw the Inspector off. Young Gillespie seemed disposed to stay behind, but Robinshaw propelled him along with the rest and then shut the door of the front room behind him.

As he passed the window, Littlejohn gave a final glance into the room. Robinshaw was standing on the rug, one arm firmly round his girl, the other drawing figures in the air as he described his brilliant feats of detection that day. Ethel's eyes were fixed on his round, red face in adoration.

Littlejohn smiled.

Well, well. If she matured into someone like her mother, no harm would be done. Robinshaw wouldn't become a second Gillespie. He'd a hide like a rhinoceros!

Littlejohn suddenly remembered that he hadn't seen Gillespie's pigeons, which he'd heard clucking and cooing as he ate his tea.

Probably Mrs. Gillespie had forbidden her husband from taking up their visitor's time with such trivialities. Anyway, Gillespie hadn't mentioned it. . . .

◆ 11 ◆

ALIBI AT THE PALACE

SO Mrs. Doakes had been at the pictures when the murder occurred. It seemed a very thin alibi and Littlejohn determined to find out just how much water it would hold.

He strolled along the promenade from Gillespie's house to *The Palace*.

It was a lovely, warm evening. The tide was in; the promenade was full of holidaymakers enjoying the air. It quite gave Littlejohn the holiday feeling. He slackened his speed, smoked his pipe and wished he hadn't to go to the picture-house at all.

A 'plane flew overhead, two speedboats skimmed across the water of the bay, leaving a trail of white behind them, and there was a film unit shooting a crowd scene on the promenade. One of the actors was surrounded by an eager herd of autograph-hunters.

A little, busy woman approached Littlejohn and, pointing at the mob round the cameras, confidentially and proudly informed him that Leslie Trumble was there and that he was a very nice boy.

"Leslie Trumble?"

Littlejohn was quite at a loss.

"Yes. Don't you know Leslie Trumble? The film star . . ."

She looked in disgust at Littlejohn's blank expression and walked away without another word, marvelling at the abyss of his ignorance.

The evangelist on the beach was hard at it. Accompanying them on a portable organ, he led his congregation, a vast one, in a hymn, which swept the promenade from end to end.

> *Sweet fields beyond the swelling flood,*
> *Stand dressed in living green,*
> *So to the Jews old Canaan stood,*
> *While Jordan rolled between.*

The film producer, who was a Jew himself, was tearing his hair and sending an underling to stem the flood of fervour and make everything O.K. for Sound. Money no object! The producer fished in the pocket of his flannel bags and gave his understrapper a five-pound note to give the evangelist to hold up Jordan for ten minutes. . . .

You could hardly get near *The Palace*. Leslie Trumble was going to make a personal appearance when he'd finished on location. The crowd of women looked ready to tear him in a hundred pieces when he arrived. . . .

Littlejohn had consulted the timetable of trains between Fetling and Stainford Junction. It was possible to sneak out of the pictures, catch the 7.45 to Stainford from Fetling, leave the train at 8.15 at Stainford and get the 8.31 back to Fetling.

Quick work, but enabling whoever did it to return to the cinema in time to make an exit past the doorkeeper with others leaving the place.

But, if Mrs. Doakes had done it, how had she got in the cinema again without being seen? As a rule, the exits of picture-houses are kept fastened, and whilst there is a safety-bar to make egress easy, it locks automatically as the door closes. She couldn't have got out and back unless someone inside had let her in when she returned.

The doorkeeper was a pompous little fellow, whose pride

at the approaching visit of Leslie Trumble almost overcame him. He was bossing about among the people in the queues outside.

"House Full; No Seats . . ." he kept shouting and strutting from end to end of the ragged lines of hopeful faces. Those in the queues were evidently anticipating some miracle or other whereby the audience inside would suddenly decide to turn out and leave them seats from which to enjoy Trumble.

The doorman's dignity was destroyed by the fact that his uniform was two sizes too large for him. His predecessor had been broader in the chest and narrower in the paunch and a dearth of clothing coupons had prevented the newcomer from getting a fresh rig-out.

"Was you wanting somethin'? No seats; house full. Go to the end of the queue if you want to stop . . ."

"A word with you," said Littlejohn.

The attendant hitched his cuffs to hide their surplus length.

"No use tryin' to square me. Not a seat in the 'ouse . . ."

"Police!" said Littlejohn.

"One of you's no good to look arter Mister Trumble when he comes. You'll need dozens. This lot'll tear 'is clothes off him, an' no mistake."

He eyed the predatory line of women like the keeper of a tiger-house at the zoo. They had laughed at him and his uniform and he was itching to get even with them.

". . . proper wild they are. I wouldn't be Mister Trumble . . ."

"Damn Trumble," said Littlejohn, and the attendant and those near recoiled in horror as though he had blasphemed in a holy place. Some of the more fanatical women looked ready to attack him.

"Come inside. This is a private matter."

The little man, endeavouring to inflate himself to fit his uniform, led Littlejohn into the porch by the pay-boxes and indicated that he was ready to listen to anything reasonable.

Yes. He had seen Mrs. Doakes come in and go out on the night of the murder. He knew her quite well. In fact, before he took on this job, he'd driven a carrier's cart and did quite a few jobs for *The Seven Whistlers,* shifting stuff about and such-like.

"Was there anybody with her?"

"No, she was by herself. Somethin' fresh, that. . . ."

"What do you mean?"

"Often as not, she 'ad a bloke with her. Husband's away at sea and she doesn't mind a bit o' congenial company now and then. . . . See what I mean?"

His upper lip shot back across his teeth like a trapdoor opening. It was supposed to be a knowing smile.

"Could she have got out at one of the exits and then come in again?"

"No. Not likely. You can get out, but you carn't come back again. Doors close and lock autermatic. If they didn't everybody'd be able to dodge in the place and get a free show. . . ."

He looked contemptuously at Littlejohn for being so innocent.

"Were you at the door all the time?"

"Yes. Except just before the show finished, I was at the door and in the vestibule. Nobody could 'ave come in or gone out without me seein' 'em."

"What about the other door?"

"That? There's no attendant like me there. That's the cheap seats. . . ."

He said it like a real snob.

"Couldn't she have come in that way a second time?"

The doorman was getting out of patience at the detective's lack of wits.

"Course not. Not unless she climbed over the balcony, let herself down one o' the pillars to get out, or shinned up one to get in. . . ."

"You mean the balcony and stalls are entirely cut off, except by access from the main door."

"That's right. The door to the cheap seats *leads* to the cheap seats and nowhere else."

"Now listen. Suppose I go in the cheap seats, can I get to the balcony without coming back into this vestibule?"

"No. The stalls and balcony's connected by steps from the front door only. And, as I said, nobody could come or go without me seein' 'em. . . ."

"Good."

The doorkeeper looked relieved.

Outside, there was a full-throated roar and the queue began to scuffle in an effort to get in the house again.

The attendant rushed out and could be seen flailing his long-sleeves among a crowd of hats and handbags. Then he returned, hot and dishevelled.

False alarm!

"They'll 'ave to call out the soldiers to quieten that lot," he said. "When Trumble does come they'll be a riot . . ."

"Never mind Trumble. Let them lynch him if they want. How many houses do you have here?"

"Continuous, except Saturday. Starts six o'clock weekdays and goes on continuous till half-ten. Saturdays, two complete 'ouses, six-thirty and h'eight-forty."

"So you can come in and go out when you like?"

"Yep!"

"Why do people queue, then?"

What a question! The doorkeeper almost spat in disgust.

"They's always a queue starts about eight o'clock for the

second showin' o' the feature film. When the first round's over a lot o' people leave and they's empty seats. . . . See?"

Littlejohn knew it all. He'd had some. Plenty. But he just wanted to check the details.

"You said just now you saw everybody coming and going except just before the show finished. What did you mean?"

"Well, it's this way. I've got to take in the glass cases with the 'stills' in 'em. You know, these things, photos of bits of the pictures . . ."

He pointed with his sleeves, which covered his entire hand, to three glass cases hanging on the outer wall near the main door.

". . . We used ter leave them out all night, but they's a lot o' sailors billeted in town now and they get to throwin' beer bottles at the pictures when they're drunk at night. So, the boss 'ad the cases made to take off. I carries them in to the boss's office every night now, just before the show ends."

"Where is the manager's room?"

The doorman pointed his sleeve to a half-open door labelled "Manager. Private." Inside, you could see autographed facsimile photographs of film-stars all over the walls.

"Where's the ladies' room?"

"There . . ."

Another door just round the corner from the main entrance.

Anybody knowing the doorkeeper's nightly routine could wait until he was busy with his cases and sneak into the ladies' room. Then, quietly creep out and mix with the crowds when the show was over, passing and bidding goodnight to the man in the ill-fitting uniform.

So much for the alibi.

But what about motive? That still eluded them.

Suddenly, a roar from inside the picture-house announced that something had happened. The doorman smiled to himself.

"What's that?"

"Leslie Trumble. They've let him in by one of the exits. Part o' the plan, see?"

Littlejohn smiled at life's ironies.

News had reached the waiting crowd outside. They were rioting. A shouting stream of women rushed the entrances, poured into the vestibule, and entered the auditorium like a great flood. They bore Littlejohn and the attendant along like flotsam. Tightly wedged among them, unable to move arms or legs, Littlejohn floated helplessly along. On the stage appeared a dark man with wavy hair, dressed in flannels and a leather golfing jacket. A wild shout of exultation with a trace of a sob in it rose from the human mass packed in the hall.

Littlejohn got jammed against one of the exits. Frenziedly he tussled with the bar, and suddenly the door opened. He found himself in the open air. So tightly packed had the audience been, that the opening of the exit ejected about twenty women with Littlejohn, like soda water leaving a syphon under pressure. The door closed, and those left outside, slowly recovering from their intoxication, realised what had happened and hared off to try and get in again by hook or crook. Through the jerry-built walls of the picture-house you could still hear the roaring of the women inside. At any time they might burst the place assunder!

Littlejohn straightened his tie and put his hat on properly. A brisk walk along the promenade would do him good after that.

The wind had freshened and there were white horses on the sea. The sun had fallen below the clouds clustered on the horizon, leaving a red flush in the western sky. Fishing boats were returning to harbour and the tide was going out.

Littlejohn leaned over the rail of the promenade and looked at the busy sea, with white breakers tirelessly pounding the shingle and tossing their white heads against the stones. He felt tired and melancholy.

Where was he? So far, his enquiries had produced very little.

First, there appeared to be complete absence of motive. Grossman seemed without enemies, and even if he had not got on too well with his business associates, there didn't seem anything that might make them wish to kill him. His own and the efforts of the police had failed to unearth any adequate reason for his death.

And all this business about breaking Mrs. Doakes's alibi at the pictures. What was the good of it? All the trouble and scrimmaging of the last hour had simply shown that she could have got in and out of the cinema without being seen. Why should she want to go out? She had no reason for wishing Grossman dead.

The same with his partner. Earlier in the day the local police had been assured by waiters and fellow drinkers that Small had spent the whole of the evening of Grossman's murder in the smoke-room of the Bay Hotel, getting himself drunk.

Barbara Curwen, too, Grossman's mistress. She hadn't shown much grief at his death, so matters were probably growing cold between them. If she'd played the part of the woman scorned, then she'd chosen a funny way of killing her former lover. It all depended on Cromwell's luck in checking her alibi and it was ten to one it would prove a satisfactory one.

The idea of suffocating a man in a box, of stitching up the sacking again, seemed, somehow, a feminine one, but you never knew. It was all a matter of expediency.

The second key, too. Well, if Miss Adlestrop had one in her bag, there was bound to be a second key, somewhere, for the box had been locked when despatched and showed no signs of forcing. Like hunting for a needle in a haystack trying to find the other key. . . .

The flag as well. Robinshaw's enquiries had drawn a blank. Anybody might have bought a flag from the rebellious, busy little woman who had determined to get rid of her stock as soon as possible.

Underlying this murder there must be some deep motive which was eluding the police. What could it be? More love affairs? Or robbery? But all Grossman's personal valuables were intact when he was found. Had he, unknown to his partner, taken some large sum of money with him for his own purposes? That might be a line worth following. On the morrow, Littlejohn would call at the bank.

The thought of the bank brought also to mind the state of Grossman's account there. Perhaps it would reveal the nature of his activities. He might even be a fence on the sly. Pity it was so late. Littlejohn was eager to pursue that line. It would have cheered him a bit. He felt he needed it.

At his elbow, a small man in a shabby, grey suit and blue cloth hat was reading the paper. He was so short-sighted that he had to hold the paper within a few inches of his eyes and looked to be sniffing and receiving the news through smell instead of sight.

He turned his large, melancholy eyes on Littlejohn.

"Gone colder . . ."

"Yes."

There was a pause.

"Been here long?"

"A few days."

"I live here. Plumbing business. . . ."

The man seemed all eyes, so hard did he struggle to see.

He paused, as though making up his mind whether or not to confide in Littlejohn.

"All this film business. . . . There's a company here taking films . . ."

Littlejohn prepared to clear off. He was tired of the film company.

The man was looking far out to sea, as if seeking a returning ship on the horizon.

"I'm fed up with it all. Upsettin' like, it is. Now, my wife's taken a fancy to one of the actors—chap called Tumble, or somethin'. Following the film lot all over the place. And she's not the only one. Barmy they've gone, the pack of 'em. For the fortnight while that lot's been here, I've had every blessed meal to get ready for myself, and wash-up after. Wife's out all the time, watchin' the films being made and admiring Tumble or whatever he's called. Turned the 'eads of all the women here, it has. It's not good enough. . . ."

Littlejohn, looking at the man's shabby dress and lack of energy, was not surprised. Inside him he was saying "No wonder . . ."

And then, turning his eyes to the man's worried face, he was full of compassion. The chap wasn't really blaming his wife. He was puzzled to know what he'd done to deserve such treatment. There was a sort of baffled humility about him, self-reproach. . . .

"Don't worry, old chap. It'll soon be over. They'll be packing their traps and off in a day or two. And then things'll be normal again. Judging from the scramble down at *The Palace,* you're not the only man whose wife's dissatisfied with him. . . . Good-night."

Littlejohn turned to find his hotel. In the distance he made out familiar forms. Robinshaw and Ethel Gillespie out for a walk. And with them, Mrs. Gillespie. Robinshaw was between his two women and looking pleased with himself, as usual. He had changed from his serge detecting suit into grey flannels and a sports jacket, and on his feet were white shoes with cloth tops. He didn't seem to care about having Mrs. Gillespie playing gooseberry, but Ethel looked as black as night about it. Mrs. Gillespie was laying down the law. . . .

Littlejohn greeted them from a distance with a wave of the hand and raised his hat. He wasn't stopping to speak with them. Enough was as good as a feast for one day with Mrs. Gillespie. Robinshaw tried to raise a bowler that wasn't there and then, quite unshaken from his usual self-satisfaction, converted the gesture into the regulation salute and passed on, talking to his two girls. . . .

Littlejohn decided that there was only one way of dispelling his melancholy before bedtime. So he hurried to the hotel, entered the telephone box and put through a trunk call to Letty, his wife.

## 12

### MONEY IN THE BANK

THE morning was cool, for it was early. The sun was dazzling already and the weather-wise were talking about its being too bright and that it might rain later on.

Littlejohn walked along the old quay and turned to climb the many steps leading to *The Seven Whistlers*. The place stood half-way up the incline, its narrow frontage tucked between two other more pretentious souvenir shops.

The door was locked, although it was past nine o'clock, the official opening-time. Littlejohn could imagine Small idling in the back room enjoying his breakfast in his trousers and shirt, with Mrs. Doakes on the other side of the table clad in a dirty wrapper. They were that sort. No wonder Grossman quarrelled with them from time to time.

A cat lay asleep in the window, among a lot of gimcrack jewellery and odds and ends of pottery and brass. The only sign of life in the place.

At the top of the steps, which he climbed to kill time, Littlejohn found himself again in the busy part of the town, the main shopping street, with the promenade running across the end of it like a letter T.

People shopping or strolling about enjoying the morning sunshine. Tradesmen's vans and private cars dashing around and some people even making their ways to ice-cream shops at that time in the morning.

"Mornin' trip round the district?"

A charabanc tout raised his eyebrows and thumbed in the direction of a motor-coach half-full of trippers.

Littlejohn walked here and there, watching the crowds, looking in shop windows and wondering what to do next.

"Charabanc trip to Angley Abbey, guv'nor. Eight and six, there an' back. Back fer lunch. . . ."

The holiday feeling was coming back over Littlejohn.

He made his way to the steps and descended to *The Seven Whistlers* again.

Mrs. Doakes had just opened the shop. She was perfunctorily dusting odd articles of furniture and ended by hoisting the cat out of the window by the scruff of the neck and throwing it into the middle of the street.

As Littlejohn had guessed, she was still in her wrapper, half-clad underneath, her hair in curling pins. She hadn't had a wash.

"What! You again?"

"Yes. Mr. Small in?"

No greetings. Just a general attitude of mutual dislike. Littlejohn didn't wait for the woman to call Small to the shop. He went straight into the living-room at the back.

Small was sitting there. Shirt, braces, trousers, bedroom-slippers with holes in the soles. He hadn't had a wash, either, and his thin fringe of hair stood uncombed round his orange-like head. An empty, greasy plate stood on the table in front of him, there was a newspaper propped up against a brown earthenware teapot, and Small was drinking a cup of tea held in both hands. He looked up and his face grew unpleasant as Littlejohn entered. He took a noisy drink and put the cup violently in his saucer.

"What the 'ell do *you* want again? Can't we have a minute's peace. Last thing at night and first in the morning —it's not damn' well good enough. . . ."

"That'll do, Mr. Small. Until we find out who killed Mr.

Grossman you're likely to keep seeing me. As soon as the crime's solved I'll be delighted to take myself off."

"No more delighted than we'll be. What do you want this time?"

Mrs. Doakes shuffled in. She was wearing mules decorated with bedraggled feathers, and no stockings. Her feet were dirty. Littlejohn looked from one to the other of the untidy couple. They returned his gaze in a sort of challenge.

It all seemed unreal. The dirty room, full of stale air. The quiet backwater with the bustle of the town shut out. Meals served anyhow. Eating, drinking and snoozing about the place. Then the bell would ring and one of them would go into the shop. Even then, not particular about whether you took it or left it. Day in, day out, sitting there getting older and fatter. Sometimes leaving to go to a sale, buying a thing or two, selling a thing or two, and then the shop was closed. Off went Small to get drunk at the Bay Hotel and Mrs. Doakes went to the pictures or picked up a boy friend for a night's relaxation. . . .

What was Grossman doing in the midst of it all? A dapper little chap, said to be fastidious and somewhat of a connoisseur in his own line. . . . Littlejohn looked at the table. Dirty pots scattered across a newspaper instead of a tablecloth. Grossman . . . ?

"Did Mr. Grossman interest himself in anything else besides this business?"

Littlejohn felt surprised at the sound of his own voice. The place was so still. Small and Mrs. Doakes waiting for Littlejohn to open the ball and on their guard. Small breathing heavily. The cat, which had returned, purring joyfully and rubbing against the table leg, and on the wall a clock with a heavy tick racing noisily. Tuck-tuck; tuck-tuck; tuck-tuck. It struck ten. Somebody must have removed the bell, for the hammer hit thin air ten times. . . .

Small picked his teeth with a match which he had whittled to a point.

"What do you mean?"

"Had Mr. Grossman any other source of income than this shop, if you care to put it that way?"

"Might have had—I dunno. Might have done a bit of dealing in glass, china and the like on the side."

"Did he spend much time here?"

"Oh, don't think I don't know what you're gettin' at. You mean how could a fussy, finicky chap like Grossman stand to be about a place like this room, eh? We're not particular folk, are we Doris? We like comfort and free and easy . . ."

Mrs. Doakes nodded defiantly.

"Well, if you must know, Grossman didn't spend any more time than he could help in this room. Went out for his meals and lived away from the place. This is mine and Doris's home, and if he didn't like it, he could lump it. He lumped it mostly. . . ."

"Had he any large sums about him when he set off for London?"

"Don't ask me. He never told me anything of his own affairs. If he'd bought in London for the firm, he'd have paid by cheque. What he did off his own bat didn't concern us. We didn't ask about what we wasn't intended to know. Did we, Doris?"

"No. He was a close fish about his private affairs. Never told us a thing. . . ."

"I see. So you can't help me on that score?"

"No. We've told you all we know. Haven't we, Doris?"

"Yes."

They kept smiling at each other like two gloating over a secret and pleased at a third party being mystified.

"Where did Mr. Grossman bank?"

"What's that to do with it?"

"Where?"

"Home Counties—in the High Street."

"Thanks. That the only place where he had an account?"

"Far as we know. We bank there for the shop as well. Don't we, Doris?"

Small kept referring to Mrs. Doakes for corroboration, which, when given, seemed to please him immensely.

He rose, and stretched himself.

"That all? Want to get a wash. . . ."

Littlejohn almost said "Time, too," but bade him good-morning instead. Mrs. Doakes bent to give the cat some milk in Small's saucer. Her wrapper parted and displayed her bosom, but she didn't seem to care. In that backwater nobody seemed to care about anything. . . .

Littlejohn was relieved to get in the street again. The air was like wine after the greasy fug of *The Seven Whistlers*. He hoped he'd finished his trips there, although he had his doubts.

The Home Counties Bank was crowded. Customers paying in their takings in the middle of a busy season. Six cashiers hard at it. And clerks running about like a lot of ants. Littlejohn entered a box labelled "Manager" and rang the handbell. A girl clerk bounced in as though she had been waiting in hiding for somebody to touch the bell.

Littlejohn sent in his card. The manager said he would see him at once.

It turned out that the manager was called Littlejohn as well. Percy Littlejohn! The two of them were very amused about it and it eased the situation considerably. They didn't waste any time trying to establish family connections.

Percy Littlejohn was tall, dark and going bald. He wore heavy, black-framed glasses, and seemed very young for the job in spite of his lack of hair. He was dressed in tweeds and a foulard tie with yellow spots, and looked to have the holiday feeling, too.

"It's very awkward," said the banker. "We're not supposed to answer questions of that sort, even if our client's dead. . . ."

Littlejohn had asked what sort of an account Grossman had kept with the bank and what the nature of the transactions might be.

"But seeing that you're one of the family, as it were . . ."

They both grinned and the Inspector decided that Percy Littlejohn might be a bit of a wag.

The manager sent for the ledger containing Grossman's account.

"Now this is strictly in confidence. I'll tell you all I can on the understanding that if you need to use the information in court you'll ask us for it again, this time with an order from the court to supply it. In other words, this is only to help you with the case and for your own use. Agreed?"

"Agreed. And I'm very much obliged to you."

The manager turned over the pages of the account and ran his finger down the columns.

"There's a good balance here. A few thousands. And a good turnover, too."

"But I'd imagine that the bulk of *The Seven Whistlers* business goes through the firm's account, not through Mr. Grossman's private one. Am I right?"

"Yes. This seems to be a cash business here. Large sums paid in, marked 'Cash,' and cheques for large amounts payable to 'Self' drawn out in cash, as well. . . ."

"What kind of cash? Could you tell me, sir?"

The manager rang for a clerk, told him what he wanted and they sat back and chatted until the information arrived.

All Grossman's dealings were in pound notes.

"What quantities, if I may ask?"

"Well, here's five hundred drawn out. Eleven hundred paid in. Then another seven hundred withdrawn—and so on. Round hundreds for the most part."

"Was there any large withdrawal a day or two before Grossman's death?"

Littlejohn gave the manager the date.

"No," replied the other Littlejohn promptly. "The last withdrawal was about three weeks ago. Twenty-five hundred pounds."

"Well, well. That's very helpful. Very helpful indeed, Mr. Littlejohn, and I'm very much obliged for your help."

"How is it helpful, Inspector?"

"Well, you've told me your secrets, I'll tell you what I think. I think Mr. Grossman was carrying on some illicit business on the sly. Unknown, perhaps, to his partners in *The Seven Whistlers*. It may have been black market. There's a lot of that now. Or, it may have been what I think it more likely . . ."

"What's that?"

"He was a fence. . . ."

"Stolen goods? By Jove!"

"Yes. The round amounts seem to point that way. Also, his business lends itself to that kind of work. Trinkets, second-hand jewels and furniture, trucking and trading all over the shop. It's an easy cover for that sort of thing."

"Well, I *am* surprised. He seemed quite a decent, harmless sort of little fellah. . . ."

"They often are. On the other hand, it may be that he's quite innocent of lawbreaking. We'll have to find out. Meanwhile, although your information's very useful, I'll see that it's kept strictly for my own use. Good-morning, Mr. Littlejohn."

"Very glad to be of any help. Call again if there's anything more we can do. Good-morning, Mr. Littlejohn."

They both laughed and shook hands.

Littlejohn called for a cup of tea at a small teashop. He wanted to sort things out and to do it quietly.

Assuming Grossman was a fence, how could that have caused his death? It certainly provided a motive at last. That motive might be robbery or revenge. Or—supposing the money paid in by Grossman had been from blackmail. An excellent motive! But who was he blackmailing?

On the other hand, those large withdrawals. Was somebody else carrying on counter-blackmail against Grossman and had they quarrelled?

It seemed more than likely that the money had been turned over in stolen property deals.

Grossman withdraws a large sum to pay for stolen goods. Right. That was borne out by the bank account. Then, whilst pretending to attend antique sales, he calls on his agent in London to get rid of the stolen stuff through the usual channels. He takes the goods with him. Jewellery, perhaps. Someone knows he has it and attacks him on the train and takes it. The criminal is disturbed. Maybe by the guard. Maybe anybody. So hides Grossman in the chest in the van nearby. . . .

But who knew that the chest was there?

The station and train staff, the carriers, Small, Mrs. Doakes. Yes, even the murderer who had followed Grossman to the train. It still might be anybody!

But who was likely to know that Grossman was carrying the stuff? Small? Mrs. Doakes? They said they knew nothing of his other activities. Small had an alibi. Mrs. Doakes had her picture-house tale, and that only.

On the other hand, the original thief who'd sold the

jewels, or whatever they might be, may have come along to get them back again.

Littlejohn drank up his tea and knocked out his pipe. As far away as ever!

They'd better start by checking up the local robberies. That would be something else for Gillespie's men. Littlejohn returned to the police station.

Gillespie was absent. It was court day and the Superintendent was prosecuting in certain cases before the magistrates. Littlejohn wrote a brief note asking him to get out particulars of recent local robberies, say over twelve months. That ought to cover everything.

"Had many big robberies around this neighbourhood of late?" asked Littlejohn of the sergeant-in-charge as he made his way out.

"Nothin' to speak of, sir," replied the man. "Bits o' petty pilferin' and such, but not what you might call any cause celebry, as you might say. . . ."

He had seen it in a book, *cause célèbre,* in connection with the Dreyfus Case, and he wanted to work it off on someone after looking it up in his daughter's French dictionary.

"Oh," said Littlejohn, and made off.

## 13

### THE APPEARANCE OF BIRDIE JAMESON

LITTLEJOHN met Gillespie in the street. He was in plain clothes, smoking a large curved pipe, and he looked very cheerful. In the course of conversation, he disclosed to Littlejohn that he was going to live a bachelor existence for the next fortnight. Robinshaw and his daughter were going away to a distant seaside resort for their annual holiday and Mrs. Gillespie had expressed the opinion that it wasn't right for them to go without a chaperone and might cause local tongues to wag. Miss Gillespie was furious and talked of calling the whole thing off. Robinshaw didn't seem to mind and he and his future mother-in-law had finally persuaded the girl to fall in with the plan. Gillespie was delighted.

"I'll bet they've a job to persuade ma not to go with 'em on their honeymoon," he said, puffing at his pipe with great relish.

Littlejohn realised that, left to himself, Gillespie might develop a mordant sense of humour.

"But that's not what I want you about, Littlejohn. I hear you were asking yesterday about local robberies. That so?"

"Yes."

"Why, might I ask?"

"Well, I'm beginning to think that Grossman was carrying on some other business that might have given a motive for the murder. It might have been blackmail. Or, he might have been a fence. In the latter event, I think perhaps local robberies, if any, might be of interest. The loot might have found its way to Grossman. What do you think?"

"Very probably. There have been one or two cases locally over the past twelve months, but the really big job was that at Coatcliffe Hall, Lord Trotwoode's place. Somebody got in there on the night of the hunt ball about four months ago, and stole Lady Trotwoode's diamond necklace, taken from the bank for the occasion."

"Did they, by gad!"

"Yes. And we got the fellow who did it only last week."

"Well, well."

"Yes. A pure stroke of luck. A well-known local bad-lot. Chap of the name of Clifford Jameson, better known as Birdie Jameson because he used to imitate bird-calls on the local halls. But he found a better way of making money. Temporarily, of course, until we laid our hands on him. He turned to cat-burgling and was damn good at it. We got him on one or two counts and he did a stretch or two as a result. We thought he'd reformed. And then the Coatcliffe job—right up his street and true to pattern. . . ."

"How?"

"Jewellery left on her ladyship's dressing-table and whilst she was out of the room—on the first floor it was—somebody lifted them. Somebody who knew the event was coming off and guessed she'd be decking herself out in her traditional finery. Somebody who knew the Hall, too, where her room was, and where to wait till the coast was clear. It was Birdie right enough."

"And why were you so long getting him? Did he run away far?"

"You might well ask. You'll laugh when I tell you. It was obviously Birdie's work and he'd been seen in the locality, but after the robbery he just vanished into thin air. Not a sign of him anywhere. All the police of the land on the look-out, but never a sign."

"Well?"

"Know where he was all the time?"

"Suppose you tell me. . . ."

Gillespie puffed his pipe with great relish and cordially returned the salute of a passing constable by raising his hat to him.

"He was found in the Army of Occupation in the Rhineland. Can you beat it?"

"What was he doing there?"

"He'd been called-up from another town and after the war found himself in Germany—Osnabrück, I think the place was. So, none of his old buddies here knew anything about him. Then he came home on leave, went to his old digs elsewhere first, togged up in his civvies, and arrived here to look up some pals. Whilst he was in Fetling he heard about the hunt ball and, being a local lad, knew her ladyship would have on the famous diamonds. He owned up to it all when he saw his goose was cooked. And do you know *why* he says he did the job? Because he was bored and wanted a bit of excitement!"

"I can quite understand him—quite. I guess the artist was craving for a change from guarding the Huns. He'd disposed of the loot, I guess."

"Yes. So he said. Held on to them for a bit and then got rid of them."

"And I don't suppose he told you where."

"Not on your life . . . He might need the fence again. Besides, these fellows have a way of getting their own back on those who betray them."

Littlejohn wished he'd brought a light suit. The sun was shining fiercely. Gillespie was in a flannel rig-out with a flower in his button-hole and all the passers-by were in holiday wear. The atmosphere of the place took hold of you. . . .

It would brighten things up if he saw Mr. Birdie Jameson.

"How did you manage to get hold of Jameson?"

"Quite by accident. We always try the Forces, of course, when we're on the hunt for a man. I don't need to tell you that."

"No, you don't."

"But Jameson had registered and joined-up as Walter instead of Clifford—reasons of his own, I guess. Very understandable ones. . . . Well, one of our constables, a chap called Fiddler, has a son in the place where Birdie was billeted and he happened to come across him by accident. Knowing his father had, one time and another, been interested in running Birdie in, he just jocularly mentioned it in a letter home. Of course, that did it. We had Birdie here by return of post, as you might say. Hu-hu-hu . . ."

Gillespie actually laughed. It was a hoarse, braying sound, and, passing through his pipe, converted it into a miniature volcano and covered his nice grey suit and red carnation with hot ash.

"And Birdie owned up to the job?"

"Yes," said Gillespie, earnestly dusting himself down and anxiously making sure that he hadn't set fire to his suit, for had he done so, his wife would have made life not worth living for him for weeks after discovering it. "You see, he was spotted about the place at the time of the robbery and the records at Osnabrück tallied with his leave time. . . ."

"Was he here when Grossman was killed, though?"

"Definitely not. You thinkin' he might have quarrelled with the little man about the proceeds. No. You can put that out of your head. Practically the whole army of occupation can swear that Birdie was in Germany at the time of the crime. You see, he was imitating birds at a Forces concert. . . ."

"Couldn't have had a better alibi, could he?"

"He could not."

"Well, I'd like to see this Birdie. Maybe he's the very thing we want to help us in this case that doesn't yield a clue or the trace of a scent."

"You shall see him at once. He comes before the magistrates this afternoon. They'll send him to the assizes, of course. But he's been brought in this morning from the county jail and is now our guest. Hu-hu-hu . . ."

He removed his pipe this time and laughed heartily. The prospects of liberty from his wife's ceaseless domination were making a new and merry man of Gillespie!

Birdie Jameson was the very antithesis of a cat burglar. He was small, tubby and cheerful. He had a bald head, too, which tapered off to a point at the top. None of the outer qualifications of a robber accustomed to shinning up drainpipes or climbing over roofs, yet a local legend for his ingenuity in finding his way to valuables up, over and through every form of obstacle.

Jameson knew of Littlejohn by reputation. He said so and greeted him like an old friend, a member of an affiliated society.

"Heard o' you," he said. "Ran-in my pal, Gus Oates. Remember Gus, Inspector? Kep' a pub at Swiss Cottage an' got too friendly with the Bert Clooes gang. Remember 'im?"

"Come to think of it, I do, Birdie. But that's not what I'm here for. . . ."

"I wasn't sayin' you was, Inspector. But should old acquaintance be forgot? What you after?"

Birdie smiled an ingratiating smile, like a shopwalker

anxious to direct a client to the right counter. His mouth was large and he had queer, long, triangular teeth, with the apexes fitting in his gums. His merry, clean-shaven, round face radiated goodwill as though he wasn't going before the bench but on a long holiday. Come to think of it, he was, wasn't he? Perhaps the prospect pleased him. . . .

"I hear you relieved Lady Trotwoode of her diamonds some time ago, Birdie."

"Who told yer that? I come before the beak to-day and I ain't said I'm pleading guilty. . . ."

"You'll be found guilty, I guess, whether you plead it or not."

"Gawd! Talk o' English justice. . . ."

"According to your statement, when they got you, you said 'It's a fair cop!' That true?"

Birdie burst into roars of laughter. His whole body vibrated like a jelly. Arms and legs as well.

"What I like about you, Inspector, if you'll pardon me sayin' it, is your 'umour. Allus admired among the fraternity for yore 'umour. Whenever there's a perfessional gathering o' me and me likes, we allus wish one another, like wishin' each other good-luck, like, we allus wish each other the 'ope that if they are pinched, Inspector Littlejohn'll do the pinchin'. Got a sense o' 'umour. Pinch yer wiv a 'umorous sally, as you might say."

"Come off it, Birdie. No more putting-off. Let's get down to brass tacks. Help me and I'll do my best for you."

"And what might that be? Goin' to say to the beaks 'Don't send pore ole Birdie to prison—'e's a pal o' mine'? Go on!"

"No. But you know the police can be useful, and if you'll give me some information I'll see you don't suffer for it. I can't say more than that."

"Well; what is it?"

"Grossman. You know he was murdered a day or two ago?"

Birdie didn't laugh this time. He grew aggressive. He needed to raise himself on his tiptoes even to reach Littlejohn's chin, but he did it and thrust his large mouth and triangular teeth savagely in the direction of Littlejohn's soft collar as though about to bite his throat.

"Yuss, I know. An' you carn't pin it on me. I got me alibi, see? An' do what you like, you can't break it. So you needn't waste any time . . ."

"Getting very heated about nothing, Birdie, aren't you?"

"Well, I thought better of you than that. Tryin' to . . ."

"Nothing of the kind. But the way you're carrying on tells me who the fence was to whom you sold those stones."

"I ain't sayin' nuffin', see?"

"But the man's dead. He's past harming you, if you've any fears on that score. He'll do no more business with you or you with him. He's dead and cremated now."

"I don't care if he's double dead an' double cremated— or triple cremated—I'm sayin' nuffin'. Nix."

"So he had a partner, had he? Who?"

Birdie Jameson's lips closed in a tight line. His little eyes twinkled defiantly and then he relaxed and started to laugh again. A real convulsion of mirth.

"I was jest larfin' at your face, Inspector. You jest look as if I'd told yer all you wanted to know. Still smilin', eh? Allus the sense o' 'umour. That's what I like . . ."

"Cut it out, Birdie. You have told me what I want to know. You sold 'em to Grossman. Let me see, seven hundred, he gave you, was it? Valued at about five thousand by the insurance people—or more. . . ."

"You don't get me that way."

"Put it another way then, Birdie. You sold the diamonds to Grossman, and his partner killed him for the loot as he was on his way to London to sell them, probably for five or even ten times what you got for them. You're afraid of Grossman's associate. He's a killer, you see. How might it be if he guessed you knew who he was? Do you think he'd rest while you were alive?"

Birdie roared again.

"Allus the 'umourist. . . . Why, you've jest told me that I'm set fer a good stretch after the local beak's done with me and sent me to the assizes."

"I wouldn't be so sure about the good stretch, Birdie. You've been so useful to the police they might . . ."

" 'ere. I pled guilty, I said, didn't I?"

"No, you didn't. You just laughed. Will you still be laughing to-morrow if you're granted bail?"

"Bail? Never 'eard of it! Who'd go bail fer me?"

"I would, Birdie, if I thought I would. Two 'umourists, you know. Birds of a feather. You would laugh, wouldn't you, if I went bail for you?"

"I'd hell as like. I plead guilty and they let me out on bail till the assizes! Don't be funny. . . ."

Birdie was beginning to sweat. His red face gradually grew putty colour and the tip of his tongue took a long, slow tour round his large lips.

"Well?"

"Right. It was Grossman."

"I thought so. And who was in with him?"

"I dunno. . . ."

"Come now. Where did you take the stuff to?"

"Grossman's flat up-town."

"You seem scared of his partner, if any. Why?"

"She's done fer 'im, hasn't she?"

"She? So it's a woman?"

"There was a woman in 'is flat that night. I never see 'er, but she was there. Must 'a just left the room as I come in. There was a cigarette burnin' in an ash-tray an' it had red lipstick on it. . . ."

"Might have been a casual caller. . . ."

"No. Somebody in Grossman's confidencks. She never passed me on the stairs as I went up, and her cigarette was there as if she'd just left it. No, if you asks me, she was in the next room while I was there."

"As I say, casual caller, tucked out of sight till you'd gone."

"No. The door between the two rooms was left open. Think he'd a done that if he'd not wanted 'er to hear?"

"There sounds sense in that. . . ."

"You betcha. And if that dame's done fer Grossman, she might do fer me. I'm not afraid o' any man. But women, that's different. When women turns killers they turns good and proper. I want none of it."

"You're sure she didn't go out by the fire-escape or something?"

"The fire-escape's on the end of the corridor, not in the rooms, in that block."

"Been casting a professional eye over the place, eh, Birdie?"

"Wot if I 'ave? Sort o' second nature, as you might say."

"I'll bet it is!"

"Anythin' else?"

"No."

"An' don't ferget. No bail fer me. 'umour or no 'umour, it 'ud be a bad joke if you did."

"All right, Birdie. No bail, then. Thanks for the information."

"A pleasure. No 'ard feelings, I hope?"

"No. Good-bye. . . ."

"Good-bye, Inspector. Got a cigarette?"

Littlejohn threw him a packet containing half a dozen.

"Keep them. Hard to get nowadays; so don't smoke 'em all at once, Birdie."

"Thanks a lot, Inspector. 'umour, that's wot you've got. . . ."

And with that they led Birdie back to his cell.

## · 14 ·

### CIGARETTE ENDS

GROSSMAN'S flat was one of three constructed on the several floors of a large house up-town. The place stood in well-kept grounds and probably the rents were high.

The dead man had occupied the ground-floor flat. The landlord held the top one himself and kept an eye on the rest. A daily help cleaned the common staircase and landings. She also kept Grossman's place tidy and clean.

Littlejohn found the ground-floor flat shut up and the curtains drawn. Grossman's lease had still two months to go and nothing had been done about a new occupant. The police had already given the roofs a thorough combing, but this had revealed nothing. Not a trace of any secret or illegal activities.

Mrs. Howell, the cleaner, was busy on hands and knees polishing the parquet of the main hall. The front door was wide open, as though to give her air to puff and blow about, for she was making snorting and groaning noises as she dragged her polisher to and fro. Littlejohn wondered what she was doing on her knees at all. But Mrs. Howell was that way. She made a great fuss and labour of everything because she was always sorry for herself and liked something to grouse about.

She looked over her shoulder at Littlejohn, gave an extra fortissimo groan to show how hard was the work, and rose to her feet. Littlejohn got quite a surprise. She must have had long legs and a short body, for although apparently of normal height when genuflecting, she extended almost to Littlejohn's length when standing upright. And she was as thin as a lath. With her hatchet face, hooked nose, small, dark eyes, pointed chin, she might have been a bird of prey waiting for its next meal.

"Well?"

"Are you Mrs. Howell?"

"Yes."

She clasped the pole of the polisher in her long hands like a quarterstaff and looked ready for all comers.

"I'm the officer in charge of the Grossman case and would like to see his rooms."

"Well, I've not got the key. The police tuck all the keys and they've not sent them back."

"I have them here, and I'll leave them with you when I go."

"Much good that'll do, because I've enough work 'ere without settin' to and cleaning up that place after all the bobbies has tramped over it with their big boots and then locked it up to go dusty and me not able to get at it. An' then not knowing where me pay was comin' from even if I did do it. . . ."

"Suppose we go and have a look. . . ."

"Oh, we can go an' have a look, but I've not got all day to be lookin'. This place is more than one's job, though them as owns it don't think so. Killin' it is. . . ."

Littlejohn opened the main door of the flat. There was a small hall, and three doors led from it.

"This is the livin' room . . ."

Mrs. Howell flung open one of the doors and rushed to the window to draw back the curtains. The sun streamed in, revealing a room furnished with taste. Good antique furniture, a few nice pictures on the walls and a bookcase of opulently bound volumes in uniform calf. The rich, blue carpet showed off the tones of the fine mahogany. In cases were silver and cut-glass, and they had an air of being in use instead of museum pieces.

Grossman had known how to do himself well!

A door in one corner led into a bedroom, furnished with equal expense and taste. Probably this was the room mentioned by Jameson as the hiding-place of the woman he suspected was with Grossman when he called with his plunder.

Littlejohn strolled round the place. The other room was a neat kitchenette, which gave access through another door to a second bedroom. A queer arrangement, but probably done to save expense when the place was converted from a house into flats.

Mrs. Howell followed close on Littlejohn's heels. With many lamentations, she pointed out where the police had disturbed the place or caused her much more work by keeping it locked.

She ran here and there, snorting, picking things up and putting them down again, flicking up the dust, indicating places on the expensive carpets where the boots of heavy constables had sullied them.

"Disgustin'! Disgraceful! 'orrible!"

"Well, I don't suppose it's much use troubling yourself about it, Mrs. Howell. The furniture and such will probably be sold and the rooms vacated."

"Locked rooms in a 'ouse isn't good for the rest of the place. Dust breeds dust and it spreads all over. . . ." said the woman with the certainty of an expert on those matters.

The local police had made a thorough job of searching through Grossman's effects, and Littlejohn didn't propose to do it all over again.

Mrs. Howell was of more interest at present.

"Did you clean this place every day?"

"Every mornin'. And I must say Mr. Grossman was a tidy little man who didn't leave me a lot of mess to clear up after 'im."

She said it with reluctance, as though resenting having little or nothing to grouse about.

". . . Different from some as I might mention not so far away."

She jerked her head back, as though someone had delivered her an uppercut, to indicate the flats above.

"Did he have many visitors?"

"Now and then. He'd bring people he 'ad dealings with from time to time."

"Any regular friends call?"

Mrs. Howell gave Littlejohn an arch look, but said nothing.

"Lady friends, Mrs. Howell?"

The good woman planted her polishing mop firmly, clasped the handle with both fists, and looked set for the day.

"I'm a dishcreet woman, I am. . . ."

"I know. I'm sure you are. But Mr. Grossman is dead. Murdered, in fact. I want to get to know all about him."

Mrs. Howell's face seemed to change. Her long, loose, upper lip had previously been tight with grievance. Now it grew soft and drawn-back, revealing a lot of long, irregular teeth. Her eyes, too, became animated, and the pleasure of having something to gossip about seemed to fatten her cheeks.

"Well. There was a woman. A regular friend as used to call a night or two a week. I see her 'ere once or twice when I stayed or come back to wash up after those disgraceful bottle parties, as they call them, held in the flats upstairs.

I'm regular Chapel, I am, and don't hold with such carryings on, but I get paid and . . ."

"Yes, Mrs. Howell. But what about Mr. Grossman's visitor?"

"Don't be so out o' patience. I was comin' to it. She used to visit him once or twice a week. Left at quite a respectable 'our. Elevenish, I'd say. What they did, I don't know. Perhaps discussed antiques, or played chess, or cards. . . ."

With a sweep of a claw she indicated the old furniture and glass, a lovely set of red and black chessmen in one of the cases, and a pack of cards on a small table. Like a lecturer giving examples.

"I wouldn't say there was any carryin's on. Seemed quite a decent little man. Not a lot o' booze about, everythin' neat and tidy as it should be. Different from . . ."

And she gave herself another ghostly uppercut to show how different were the riff-raff up above.

"I'd be the last to make suggestions. . . ."

"I'm sure you would, Mrs. Howells."

"Howell—no S. . . ."

"Sorry. You knew Mr. Grossman's lady friend?"

"Yes."

She didn't say who it was and shut her mouth tight, as though wishing to maintain the suspense through her own good time.

"Miss Curwen?"

Mrs. Howell looked very annoyed. She didn't like being forestalled.

"If you know, why ask me?"

"You cleaned up this place on the day Mr. Grossman met his death?"

"I did. Pore little man."

If she was sorry, she didn't show it. Her face was like a mask.

"Anything unusual? I mean, glasses to wash, cigarette ends, cigar-butts?"

"No. Not as I reckerlect."

"Did Mr. Grossman's lady friend smoke?"

"Yes. That's 'ow I always knew she'd been here. He didn't smoke, himself. Now, she smoked cigarettes as smelled different. Nearly like cigars, they was. Place stank of 'em the day after. I used ter open the windows wide, it 'ung around so much. . . ."

"Turkish or Egyptian?"

"Arabian Nights o' some sort."

"Hm."

"An' always red lipstick on them. Faugh! Lipsticks! I've no use for such like. . . ."

"I'm sure you haven't."

"No."

"And you don't remember any other visitors, Mrs. Howell?"

"No. I'm rarely here at nights. With Miss Curwen bein' more or less regular and the tenants upstairs talkin' about 'er and 'im, I jest knew of 'er."

"That'll be all, then, Mrs. Howell. And thanks for your help."

Littlejohn gave the woman half-a-crown, which she pocketed with great nonchalance and no thanks, like an elephant taking a bun.

"The police asked me to leave the keys with you now. They've finished with the place."

"I don't know what to do with them. They don't expect me to clean up after 'em, do they, and 'im dead?"

"No, I don't think so. Those are your set, I believe, and you may as well have them. The set that belonged to Mr. Grossman will be handed over to his solicitors."

"Who are they? I've not been paid all me dues. . . ."

"I don't know. I suggest you ask the police—or I will for you. Is there a telephone?"

Mrs. Howell indicated a small cupboard in the vestibule. "There. . . ."

Littlejohn telephoned Gillespie for the information Mrs. Howell needed. Then he asked him to find out from Birdie Jameson if the cigarette he found burning was an oriental one.

There was a pause.

"Yes. Jameson's just been remanded to the assizes and he seems very pleased there's no bail. What he's bothering about bail for, I can't think. As if . . . You seem amused! By the way, he says the flat stank of Egyptian cigarettes when he called."

"I think it was Barbara Curwen who was there at the same time as Birdie. I'll be seeing you as soon as I can get to the station. We'd better get hold of that lady again and see what she has to say for herself."

Having left Mrs. Howell as satisfied as possible, Littlejohn made his way to meet Gillespie.

The Superintendent was out, but had left a message with the station sergeant that Littlejohn was to meet him at the town mortuary.

"Why, what's been happening?"

"They found a body washed up on the rocks at low tide and the Super's hurried round with the doctor to have a look."

"Anyone I'd know?"

"Maybe, sir. Friend o' the late Mr. Grossman, as you might say. Miss Barbara Curwen, sir . . ."

## · 15 ·

### DEATH ON BLIGHT HEAD

IT was very difficult to form any idea of how Barbara Curwen had met her death. She had been found on a small beach at the foot of Blight Head, a rocky headland jutting into the sea and forming the northern extremity of Fetling Bay.

The river entered the sea just off the headland, where currents were always strong and crossed. Anything thrown in the river higher up gathered and swirled around the Head and at low tide there was a heavy deposit of rubbish on the rocks there.

Miss Curwen's body might have been washed down the river and simply left for somebody to find at the ebb.

A man, hunting for crabs, it seems, had come upon the corpse and given the alarm at once.

The doctor was unable exactly to give the cause of death; which was not to be wondered at. The head was badly battered, apparently from being pounded by the currents against the rocks. Time of death was about eight or nine o'clock the previous night.

So, it might have been suicide or murder. Barbara Curwen might have thrown herself over the cliff at Blight Head out of despair. First her father had died; then her best friend. She might have done it from worry . . .

Or, again, someone might have struck her on the head

and thrown the body in the river, whence it had found its way to the spot where the river cast its burdens before joining the sea.

Gillespie took Littlejohn to the place where they had found the body. Two policemen were there, still questioning the crab-hunter who had raised the alarm. He was gesticulating freely, pointing to the rocks, to the pools where he got crabs, out to sea where the river slowly mingled with the salt water. A little, nondescript man, highly excited and full of self-importance because the limelight of publicity had already fallen upon him. The newspaper men had just been quizzing him and one of them had taken his photograph.

The ambulance had carried the body away, of course, but there was still a crowd of idlers and holidaymakers with nothing to do staring at the rocks and trying to overhear what the officials were saying.

"Come on, there's nothing more to see. Dinner'll be cold when we get to the digs . . ."

A little man in a straw panama and white shoes gathered his family together. The youngest wanted to stay on and started to howl. Their departure seemed to be the signal for the rest to make off, and gradually the spectators melted away.

A busy reporter in a raincoat was taking notes and talking to the policemen.

"You the Scotland Yard man?"

"Yes."

"Any theories?"

"No."

Littlejohn led Gillespie off.

"Nothing much we can do here. I'd better see what's happening at Miss Curwen's flat and try to find out her movements last night."

"Good idea. Any line you'd like us to follow?"

Gillespie was very morose again.

"Yes. You might find out where Small and Mrs. Doakes were at the time of the crime. . . ."

"Hullo! Still on that tack?"

"Yes. The only line to follow as yet."

"Right. I'll put a man on at once."

"You'll probably find it's the same old tale. Small boozing before everybody's eyes at the Bay Hotel; Mrs. Doakes at the pictures. . . ."

Later, it turned out that was the case.

Barbara Curwen had by this moved all her belongings into her new flat; so Littlejohn made his way there.

As he passed the picture-house he saw the overclad commissionaire busily hanging the cases of stills on hooks in front of the building.

"Good morning."

"Good mornin', sir. Managed to get safely out of the scrum the other night?"

"Yes, by the skin of my teeth. Was Mrs. Doakes here again last night?"

"Yes. Change of pictures. I saw 'er come in for the first house."

"Alone?"

"Yes. And another thing. After what you said the other night, I kep' me eyes open. Watched for her comin' out. She came out all right. But she joined the crowd from the ladies' room, just as you said. . . ."

That did it! She'd used the same plan twice!

If only they could trace Barbara Curwen's steps to *The Seven Whistlers*. As likely as not, the police questioning had aroused Miss Curwen's suspicions and she had faced Mrs. Doakes with the murder and met the same fate as Grossman.

But there was no help forthcoming at Miss Curwen's flat. The silly little maid was still there, wild-eyed, dishevelled, not knowing whether she was on her head or her heels.

"I was out all last night. My night off," she snivelled. "I left Miss Curwen here, listenin' to the wireless, waitin' for Miss Teare. She seemed all right. Been a bit worried some way, but told me nothing. What am I goin' to do?"

"Be quiet, Lucy. I've told you I'll look after you. Stop fussing. You're only sorry for yourself. Now be off to the kitchen. . . ."

That from Miss Teare, who was there when Littlejohn arrived. A large, swarthy, flat-footed woman of middle-age, dressed in tweeds and enormous brogues. She tramped heavily here and there, masterfully trying to take the situation in hand.

"Suicide! Rubbish!!" she said in answer to Littlejohn's question. "I'll admit she was a bit too friendly with that little Grossman. I never liked him myself, by the way. But not so much as to throw herself into the sea because he happened to get himself murdered. If you ask me, she'd found out something about how Grossman was killed and poked her nose in where she shouldn't have gone. . . ."

"Were you intimate with Miss Curwen, Miss Teare?"

"Her best friend. We golfed together. We should have gone to the cinema last night, but when I called, she was out. I suppose she went off on this errand while she was waiting for me and . . ."

Miss Teare didn't seem greatly moved by the tragedy. Or, if she was, she kept it bottled up inside her. Her heavy poker-face retained its indignant lines. Perhaps she hadn't got over being kept hanging about for two hours by Barbara, who'd got herself murdered instead of going to the pictures with her. . . .

"Did you know Mr. Grossman?"

"Yes. Met him at Barbara's old place a time or two. Never took to him. Slimy little chap, I thought. But Barbara seemed to like him. It was her own affair."

"She never took you into her confidence about the matter, then?"

Miss Teare's large nose twitched and her heavy nostrils dilated.

"Never mentioned him. I once told her I didn't like the fellow and we had a bit of a row, so I never raised it again. She's brought this on herself. If she'd followed my advice . . ."

Even with the two parties to the affair dead, Miss Teare was still jealous of them it seemed.

"How long were you here last night, did you say?"

Miss Teare looked moved for the first time. She started and gave Littlejohn a nasty look. Her ugly face screwed up into hard wrinkles and she planted her large brogues firmly on the carpet.

"I was here from half-past seven to half-past nine. But I don't see what it's got to do with you."

"Perhaps you don't, Miss Teare. But I'm not asking questions for the fun of it. What did you do?"

"I sat and read a magazine, listened to the radio, helped myself to a drink, and then cleared off in disgust. You're not insinuating that I had anything to do with Barbara's death, are you? Because, if you are, I'll soon have you put in your place. My father's on the County Council and I'll see that . . ."

"Don't get excited, Miss Teare. These are purely routine enquiries. I'm sure you're as anxious as we are to get to the bottom of your friend's death."

"Of course I am. But I don't know anything about it."

There was a look of feverish intensity in Miss Teare's eyes. Littlejohn wondered what it was all about. Perhaps she had fancied Grossman, too, and been jealous of her friend. You never know. . . .

Littlejohn decided to leave the Curwen affair for the time and turn to Grossman again. Probably the solution of the first crime would bring that of the second in its wake.

At Fetling station he sought details of motive and method of attack. The latter was quickly explained.

The platforms were closed ones. Anyone joining a train had to show a ticket to the man at the barrier.

Mr. Fludd was not on duty and his assistant, a pleasant, red-faced man with a flower in his buttonhole and a dandified way of dressing, including a pair of kid gloves which he carried in his hand, was very helpful. He was called Mr. Gladstone and kept humming nervously when he was not talking. He was in the chapel choir and they were shortly giving Haydn's *Creation*. He couldn't get *The Heavens Are Telling* out of his head.

"Yes. I recollect Charlie Traviss was on duty at the barrier that night. He's there again now, so we'll be able to find out just what happened. . . ."

Slapping his thighs with his gloves, Mr. Gladstone led his visitor to the barrier of platforms 1 and 2.

The loudspeakers were announcing the next train to Birmingham. About twenty stops, and the announcer recited them all until he was out of breath. He shouted them so loudly that the trumpets almost fell from their moorings with the vibration. Nobody seemed to heed his messages, for you could see people asking the porters what time the next train went for Birmingham or intermediate stations.

Mr. Traviss at the barrier was a very bad-tempered man. He regarded everyone who passed his watching-post as an antagonist anxious to dodge on a train without showing a ticket, and insisted in scrutinising and clipping every one.

Queues mounted up like water at a dam on his side of the barrier as he did his duty by his employers.

Mr. Traviss seemed happy to close his little gate and force his would-be clients to surge upon his colleague at the second barrier.

"Yes," he told Littlejohn, "Mr. Grossman passed through my barrier on his way when he met his death."

He clashed his picket punch as though challenging Littlejohn to get past if he could without a ticket of some sort.

"Did Mrs. Doakes come on with him?"

"No. I was on the job by myself and she'd not have got past without me seeing 'er. I'd have remembered. Good memory, I have. . . ."

A man with a suit-case as big as himself tried to get past Littlejohn to the platform and was loudly and angrily warned off by Traviss.

"This is closed. Go to the other side. Carn't you see?"

"Did you see Miss Curwen on the earlier train?"

"Yes. Clipped her first-class ticket. That's right. I don't forget these things. My job not to do. . . ."

Littlejohn couldn't see much claim to virtue in it, but let it pass.

"I'd just like a look along the platform, then . . ."

Mr. Gladstone waved his gloves airily at Traviss, who opened his gate with reluctance and let them through. A mob of returning holidaymakers tried to follow, and Mr. Traviss set about them, put them in their places and started to clip their tickets meticulously. You could hear his bullying voice all along the platform.

Littlejohn, directed by the deputy-stationmaster, walked along the London platform, and whilst Mr. Gladstone got on with his *Heavens Are Telling*, now whistling it, now crying it aloud in a muffled tenor, sized-up the situation.

Beyond where the trains and engines stood was a goods-yard, with sheds and cattle-pens. From the pens ran a cemented track to a gate, which in turn gave on to the main road. Evidently drovers were in the habit of using this for livestock brought in by goods train. The gate was made of metal bars and could easily be climbed. Anybody agile enough and careful to keep out of sight could sneak along the track to the far side of the train standing at the London platform and get aboard without being seen.

But the guard had checked tickets just after the train started. What about that?

Littlejohn interrupted the oratorio to ask Mr. Gladstone about it.

"Let's go to the ticket office, Inspector. Perhaps they'll be able to help."

The booking-clerk had a long queue at his peep-hole, but he was glad to close down the shutter and keep them all waiting a bit longer. If they didn't get the next train they could catch the one after that!

He wore a tattered office jacket with pins sticking from the lapels, and was tall, emaciated and weak at the knees, as though worn out from ceaseless contention with travellers. He had two other colleagues and they all swore, one by one, that Mrs. Doakes hadn't been near the ticket-office for months. Yes, they all knew her. She was well-known in the town. One of the clerks sniggered suggestively and for the first time Mr. Gladstone looked annoyed and stopped smiling and humming.

"Let's try the goods depôt and enquire about the box," said Littlejohn, and Mr. Gladstone cheerfully assented and led him off to offices on the far side of the station.

The place was a hive of industry. Boxes, crates, sacks and suitcases all over the shop and men hauling them here and there without any apparent plan of action. Two stocky little chaps were throwing parcels marked "Fragile" from one end of the room to the other as though anxious to test the veracity of the statement on the red labels.

The chief clerk was singled out by Mr. Gladstone, who was now whistling something about the fowls of the air and the fish of the sea, and left with Littlejohn whilst the stationmaster dealt with his livestock.

The clerk looked tired out, and his black alpaca jacket and dark, shiny trousers accentuated the pallor of his sad face.

"Yes, I remember the trunk. Quite a sensation it's caused, hasn't it? But we'd nothin' to do with that here. Just passed through our hands in the normal course."

"It was a box, not a trunk."

"Oh, yes. We get so many. I forgot. I do recollect it was a bit delayed in being sent. Should have gone on the passenger train before Mr. Grossman's, but there was a bit of a hitch."

"Why passenger train?"

"Better than goods for delicate stuff. Not so much goes by passenger and it doesn't get hanging about so long. And not handled as much. . . ."

You could hardly hear yourself speak for noise. Men shouting and men tabulating stuff.

"Four cases Birmingham; three cases Willesden Junction; six Norwich; five Newcastle . . ."

And Mr. Gladstone waiting amiably for Littlejohn, beating time with his gloves and singing *sotto voce* about flocks and herds.

"And now about the hitch you said occurred. What was that?"

The clerk pulled a cigarette twisted like a question-mark from his pocket, straightened it, lit it at a gas light, and puffed the smoke in Littlejohn's face.

"Sorry," he said, beating the air before the Inspector's

nose. "The box came and should have gone by the London train before the one Grossman was on. But just before it was loaded the insurance company 'phoned to ask us to leave it a bit. They was settling some point about the insurance. . . ."

"Which company was it?"

"Travellers' and Traders'."

"May I use your 'phone, please?"

The Travellers' and Traders' agent told Littlejohn that Mrs. Doakes had called on him to arrange about insurance of the box and had squabbled about the premium.

"It was something and nothing," he said, "but she kicked up a lot of fuss. A proper bitch of a woman, if you ask me."

"Indeed!" said Littlejohn in his nastiest tone. He thought of his own bitch at home, fretting and off her food when he was away, and objected to the word as an epithet. "I don't want Mrs. Doakes's character, thanks."

"No offence, I'm sure, sir. Well, Mrs. Doakes asked me to tell the railway to hold up the box till she'd seen Mr. Small about the premium, which I did. It went by the 7.45 instead of the 5.2. Later she paid up and no more fuss."

"Thank you. Goodbye."

"Wait a bit . . . Is there goin' to be a claim? I hope not."

"No claim, thank you."

Someone announced cups of tea were ready and the place emptied. A great silence prevailed. A man flung down a case marked "Handle with Care" with a resounding crash and went off for refreshment, and Mr. Gladstone looked enquiringly at Littlejohn, mutely asking if he'd had enough.

Littlejohn nodded, thanked Mr. Gladstone, who flicked his gloves to indicate that it was no trouble at all. They said goodbye, the stationmaster patted his flower, slapped himself with his gloves again and went off whistling something about creeping things.

In the distance, the red beard of Mr. Fludd could be seen coming on duty. Littlejohn turned down a side-street to avoid it and made for the police station. He was feeling happier, for whilst the facts were still a bit confused, things were beginning to take shape.

## ⸺ 16 ⸺

### THE ROOM ABOVE THE SHOP

IT was seven in the evening. Littlejohn was sitting in Gillespie's room at the police station waiting for his colleague. In the absence of his wife, Gillespie, freed from domestic routine, seemed to be wandering here, there and everywhere.

The room was very depressing and the outlook on to the grim stone church with its dreary graveyard was even worse. The office was dismally furnished with an old desk, three wooden chairs, two new filing cabinets and a cracked washbowl in one corner. They had long intended building a new place, but the war had held things up.

The church tower opposite took away a lot of the light and on all but sunny days the desk lamps had to be on. These were tiring to the eyes in spite of their green shades.

Littlejohn had been jotting down one or two notes on a piece of scrap paper.

Mrs. Doakes boards London train after sneaking from cinema without being seen by anybody.

Hides on 7.45 and attacks Grossman; conceals body in chest; returns by changing trains at Stainford; hides in ladies' room of cinema whilst attendant is changing "stills." Then, emerges from ladies' room when show ends, mixes with crowd and takes care to greet attendant to establish alibi of sorts.

Where did she hide on train, as nobody seems to have

seen her about and she didn't encounter the guard? And why all the fuss about getting the box on the same train as Grossman?

She hid in the box, of course. She had been responsible for stitching it in the canvas. A few twists of the needle, easily undone, would be enough. Then the chest could be used for concealing the body long enough to give her breathing space.

Littlejohn read through his notes again, laid down his pencil and yawned.

What a case! And all his notes were pure surmise. The woman might not have left the cinema at all. However, the doorkeeper had seen her putting into action the trick Littlejohn had imagined, on the night Barbara Curwen died. So that added strength to his theories.

The woman had certainly used her head in the crime and kept herself well concealed and planned it very precisely. None of the station officials had seen her about the place when Grossman was in the train.

The fatal box was still at the police station. Littlejohn went and examined it again. What wouldn't he have given for one of the classical clues! A thread from a coloured dress or jumper, an imprint on the bottom of a pair of number 7 shoes, or a distinctive sole, a fingerprint or a thread of golden hair!

There was nothing. Mrs. Hollis, in her anxiety to get the smell of death, as she called it, out of the box, had made a thorough job of cleaning it up.

Littlejohn put on his spectacles again and resumed his writing.

Motive?

There was something there to work on. He wrote down:

Grossman seems to have bought, in his capacity as fence, the proceeds—mostly diamonds—of the Coatcliffe burglary from Birdie Jameson. Had Mrs. Doakes got wind that the jewels were in his possession and attacked and relieved Grossman of them on his way to London to dispose of them?

And did Barbara Curwen know of the jewellery, and had she tackled Mrs. Doakes and accused her of murder?

Littlejohn yawned again. The case was boring him. The number of dead-ends was becoming exasperating. He must make a bold move or he looked like being at it for ever.

The door opened and Gillespie entered. He was in uniform and looked tired out.

"Hullo, Littlejohn. I've just been trailing round trying to find out anything interesting from Barbara Curwen's friends. No good."

Littlejohn took another chair, and as Gillespie sat down at his desk, pushed across to him the notes he had been making.

Gillespie read through them, his brow wrinkled and his fingers drumming on the desk.

"You seem to have fastened on Mrs. Doakes. But as far as I can see we've no excuse for questioning her further, let alone definitely accusing her."

"No. I was just thinking, when you came in, I must make a bold step. There's only one thing to do. Search Mrs. Doakes's room at the shop."

"Search warrant?"

"Not on your life. That would defeat our purpose. So far, our enquiries about her have been very discreet and general. If we spring the trap too soon she may get startled and get out of it. No, I'm going to make an illegal search."

Gillespie jumped, and looked startled.

"Not breaking-in?"

"Exactly. We may find the missing key, or something else that will clinch the matter. We can't go on like this for ever."

"Yes, but think of the risk. If we're found out it'll break us."

"Not you, Gillespie. This is my affair. All the help I want from you is your silence about it and for you to order the policeman on patrol on the quayside to telephone me when Small and Mrs. Doakes are out later this evening."

"All very irregular. Still, I'm between the devil and the deep sea. The Chief Constable's in a rare tear about the case. Very well. Do as you wish. . . ."

At nine o'clock that night the constable on the quay reported that *The Seven Whistlers* was deserted.

The property on the hill had once been substantial residences and there were still neglected back-gardens behind the shops. The Inspector, unaccompanied, entered the premises from this direction. He made short work of the lock on the back door and was soon inside.

There was a gas-lamp right in front of the shop and this shining through the bottle-glass threw an aqueous green light over everything inside. The antique furniture stood in solid dark masses, with the old glass shining almost as though illuminated from within in some way. Little figures of Dresden shepherds and shepherdesses danced in the moonlight and the Toby jugs grinned down grimly and the pot dogs watched like things on guard.

Three grandfather clocks ticked a sort of trio and one struck three although it was not that time at all.

Littlejohn cautiously climbed the creaking stairs. There were three doors on the landing. The first he opened proved to be a storeroom; the second was obviously Small's. The bed had not been made, the bedclothes were littered about in tangled heaps and the air was still fuggy as though the occupant had only just left it after spending a night there with the window closed.

Mrs. Doakes's room overlooked the steep street and was

over the shop. It was of the bed-sitting-room variety, with a few choice pieces of furniture acquired in the course of trade. Heavy mahogany bed and wardrobe, with dressing-chest and wash-stand to match. The bed had been made this time and the place was tolerably tidy. The lamp outside illuminated the room, but Littlejohn used his shaded torch to see in the corners.

The search was disappointing. Not a letter; not a photograph, except one of Doakes himself; or presumably it was Doakes, for he wore officer's uniform. Not a trace of money or weapons. In short, nothing connected with the crime.

Littlejohn carefully went through drawers, wardrobe and cupboards. He gently examined the bed and mattress. No loose floorboards. Apparently no secret hiding places.

Disgusted, the Inspector prepared to leave and try some other idea. He switched off his torch and stood at the window looking down at the empty street. It was very quiet. Not a soul about. In the distance you could hear the hum of the town and the noises of the boats at the quay loading and unloading. Cranes still working and men shouting. . . .

There was a soiled raincoat on the back of the door. Littlejohn had searched the pockets of all the garments in the place except this one. He eyed it without interest, but instinctively ran his fingers over it.

A half-empty packet of cigarettes, a bit of lipstick, some halves of picture-house tickets. Then, screwed up in the corner of one pocket, a receipt for a registered packet. The date of the receipt was the day after the crime!

Mr. John Doakes, c/o G.P.O., Liverpool.

Probably sending money to the port for her husband before he arrived or embarked.

Or . . .

Littlejohn was startled from his glow of satisfaction by

the sudden ringing of a bell. Someone was entering the shop by the front door! And with assurance, for whoever it was didn't mind the bell jangling. . . .

It must be either Small or Mrs. Doakes.

The heavy steps crossed the shop and made straight for the staircase. Littlejohn looked at the window of the room. Large frames which didn't open and small panes at the top, one of which had a hinged part, for ventilation. No way out there.

He was properly trapped and would have to make the best of it.

Almost before the Inspector had time to place himself behind the door, the handle turned. Small, in raincoat and cloth cap, entered. He wasn't drunk this time and evidently had an end in view. He, too, was going to search Mrs. Doakes's room.

Fortunately, Small, in his haste, didn't bother to close the door, and Littlejohn stood concealed by it, hardly daring to breathe.

It was amusing to see the huge, heavy-breathing man trying to be gentle in his search so that Mrs. Doakes wouldn't find out someone had been there. He seemed all fingers and thumbs, and grunted and talked to himself as he concentrated on the job in hand. An odour of whisky began to fill the room.

Outside, the heavy tread of the constable on patrol sounded in the street. Small paused, went to the window and watched him pass from behind the curtains.

Littlejohn swore to himself. Why didn't the fellow try the door, as probably he did on every other night whenever he passed? That would perhaps be unlocked and take Small down to explain. But no. The bobby tramped on, quite oblivious of the trouble brewing right overhead.

What was Small after? Was it the diamonds? Or the second key? Or even proof that Mrs. Doakes was somehow involved in the death of his late partner?

Small was getting mad. The fruitless search was tiring his patience and he began to chuck things about in drawers and cupboards, and then, recollecting what he was doing, had to set about tidying them again.

Having finished with the cupboards and drawers, the fat man started on the wardrobe. He merely ran his hands down the garments. He must have been after something bulky.

Then he started on the furniture. Tapping, twisting, pressing it here and there with his fingers. Evidently hunting for secret receptacles. And when he found none, he set about the bed in a very evil humour. You could see he wanted to throw the bedding about and slit the mattress, but daren't. . . .

Finally, Small drew back, breathing heavily, and pushed his cap on the back of his head.

"Where the hell are they?" he asked himself.

So, he was probably after the diamonds, too.

Suddenly, Small seemed to decide to give it up as a bad job and left the room and closed the door without even looking behind it. Littlejohn heard him stump down the stairs and go in the living-quarters behind the shop.

Then, Mrs. Doakes turned up. She mustn't have been to the pictures. The shop doorbell jangled again and you could hear her asking Small what had brought him home so early.

From where he was, with the door ajar, Littlejohn could hear Small saying he hadn't been feeling well and had come home to make himself some tea and get to bed.

The Inspector wondered which room was the safer. Mrs. Doakes might come up to powder her nose or something. She didn't look like one who went early to bed and had called to titivate herself for another appointment of some kind. Probably an amorous one!

Littlejohn decided to chance it, and softly moved across to the lumber-room.

Voices were raised.

Small, enraged by his futile search, was evidently furious. And more furious still at the early return of his niece.

"What have you done with them sparklers that Grossman had?"

"What are you babbling about?"

"You know what I'm babblin' about. Birdie Jameson's been pinched for the Coatcliffe robbery. An' you know as well as I do that Grossie always took his stuff. . . . Where are they?"

"I know nothing about any diamonds."

"Oh yes, you do. You know as well as I do that Grossie had them sparklers when he went for the London train. Or if you don't, yer a bigger mutt than I thought yer. What had he to go to London for at this time o' year? No sales, and the end of season."

"I know nothing about it."

"Don't come that over me. I bet you was after them diamonds like a cat after cream. Where was you when Grossie caught his packet?"

"At the pictures. I've got a proper alibi there, and the police took it proper, too."

"Tell it to the marines. . . ."

Then they started a regular round of abuse. Littlejohn had never heard a woman with such a vocabulary of foulness as Mrs. Doakes when she was roused. Small lost every round. In the end, he gave it up.

"And now I'm going out again. . . ."

Mrs. Doakes ran upstairs and into her room. She was on the landing in less than a minute.

"Hey! Have you been in my room?"

Small sounded astonished and outraged.

"No. Why?"

"You have, you lyin' swine. Somebody's bin through the drawers, I'm sure o' that, and the bed's not like when I left it. You dirty . . ."

"That'll do. I'm not so well and I've 'ad about enough o' you, see? Any more and I'll put you in bed for a week. I'm doin' no more talking. Fists is what I'll use."

"I'd like to see you touch me. . . ."

She was evidently in a hurry and ran downstairs, yelling abuse all the way.

"Not that I've anythin' I want to hide in my room. But my room's mine, and private, see, and I won't 'ave you messin' round there, puttin' yer dirty maulers all over my things. . . . What are you after, anyhow?"

"I tell yer I haven't been there."

"Liar!"

It sounded like starting all over again. But instead, Mrs. Doakes hurried out and the jangle of the shop-bell speeded her on her way.

Littlejohn was fed up. It looked as if he'd have to wait for Small either to go out again or retire to his room, before he could bolt.

Matters came to a climax quicker than Littlejohn expected. Small remained quiet for a time and then ascended the stairs again. And he went into Mrs. Doakes's room and gave it another good searching! The fellow was certainly persistent. Littlejohn stood listening behind the lumber-room door, holding on to some old clothes hanging on the back of it and wondering if he was going to be there all night.

Swearing to himself, Small finally let himself out of the woman's room, but instead of going to his own, opened that in which Littlejohn was hiding. And he began to fumble for the switch. . . .

Littlejohn had had quite enough. Quickly, he whipped

one of the coats down from behind the door and, flinging it over Small's head, neatly tripped him and pitched him among a heap of junk lying nearby. Then he flew down the stairs and out by the front door as fast as his legs would take him.

He tidied himself up on the way back to the police station and entered Gillespie's room with his precious post-office receipt.

Gillespie grinned at him.

"Hullo! So you're safely back, eh? Thought we'd lost you for good. I've just had a 'phone call from *The Seven Whistlers*. Seems they've had burglars and one of 'em attacked Small. Like to go down and see what it's all about?"

"No, thanks," said Littlejohn.

And the Superintendent burst into roars of loud laughter.

' 17 '

## THE "MAID OF MORVEN"

LITTLEJOHN decided to go to Liverpool right away. He telephoned to the police there and they were not long in finding out who and where was John Doakes. He was second-officer on the *Maid of Morven*. She was still in the river, held up by the dockers' strike. Otherwise, she'd have been half way to South America.

The Inspector caught the 12.30 to Liverpool from Fetling and hoped to get some sleep in the train. He only dozed, however, for he had an uneasy impulse that somehow things weren't turning out as he expected.

Why, on this of all nights, had Small suddenly decided to return home from his usual evening's drinking at the Bay Hotel at the precise time that he himself was searching the place? It seemed more than a coincidence.

The case itself had been a slow one and full of surprising twists, and Littlejohn had an uncomfortable feeling that somehow he was even now on a fool's errand.

He was right!

His theory had now developed to the extent of deducing that Mrs. Doakes had killed Grossman, perhaps by mistake, but killed him all the same. Then, she'd stolen the diamonds, and now, after receiving them by registered post, her husband was taking them to South America with him for disposal. A very pretty and handy scheme. A visit to Doakes unexpectedly might clear the whole thing up. Littlejohn vaguely felt it wouldn't.

Enquiries by the police in Fetling showed that John Doakes hadn't put in an appearance in Fetling at all during the time his ship had been docked. Why had he kept away? Perhaps to keep himself from suspicion in connection with Grossman's death, and perhaps to remain as far away as possible from the scene of the crime with the loot.

Littlejohn kept turning it over and over in his mind on the way to Liverpool.

There were three other men in the compartment. Two were drunk and on their way home from a football match. They were rowdy whilst awake and snored loudly when asleep. The third passenger fidgeted the whole of the time. Crossing and uncrossing his legs, easing his body in his seat and every time he moved agitating the whole of the side on which he and Littlejohn were sitting. And some vandal had pulled away a part of the door-frame, which let in a smoke-scented draught. Finally, when his travelling companions were all asleep, Littlejohn couldn't get off himself. His thoughts on the crime were very disturbing. He felt as though someone were leading him up the garden path, and try as he would to dismiss the ridiculous idea, he found it recurring over and over again.

A police sergeant met Littlejohn at Liverpool in the small hours. They went straight down to the docks. They found Doakes was still ashore. The boat was due to sail on the morrow and a lot of the men had been having a final fling.

Doakes returned at six o'clock, very much the worse for wear. He had slept off his drink somewhere but was in a vile temper. His clothes were crumpled, he hadn't had a wash or a shave and his collar was soiled and all shapes.

"What the hell do you two want?" he asked in what appeared to be righteous indignation. "It's come to something when a chap's disturbed by coppers at six in a morning and he hasn't done anything."

"We'd like a word with you, Mr. Doakes, in connection with the death of Mr. Grossman, for whom your wife works in Fetling."

"You would, would you? And what have I to do with things in Fetling? Haven't been there for six months."

"Why?"

"What the hell's that to do with you?"

"Keep a civil tongue in your head, Doakes. Your wife is closely connected with the crime, being in Grossman's employ. We're checking on every angle and you come into it as her husband. Where were you when the crime was committed?"

Littlejohn gave him the time, date and such particulars as were needed in the matter.

"Well, if you must know, I was in hospital. The day before the murder, I was superintending some deck operations and broke my thumb. . . ."

He held up the offending member. It was still in plaster of Paris with a strong wire loop projecting from the end of the bandage.

". . . I had it X-rayed and they found what they call a Bennett's fracture. Whatever that may be. . . . They kept me in bed at the hospital for a couple of days while they got it set proper, and then I'd to report every day for treatment. Risk of the thumb shortening, they said, if it was mismanaged. You can check that with the General Hospital. They'll tell you. So that let's me out. And now I want some sleep. . . ."

"Just a minute. It seems strange that you didn't go over to see your wife all that time. You didn't, did you?"

"No. And it's no flaming business of yours."

"Did she come to see you?"

"No. Why should she? She gets on quite well without me and I get on very well without her. . . ."

"All the same, you keep in touch—you write to one another, I mean?"

"Oh, I send her a postcard now and then. Just to let her know I'm still alive and then she'll not be getting married again to one or another of the blokes she has in tow. Wouldn't do for her be gaoled for bigamy. . . ."

"She wrote to you the day after the murder, though."

"Look here. I'm a patient man. But when I get mad I've a devil of a temper. I've not slept all night, and I've got an idea that my temper's not at its best at this early hour. So, I'll trouble you to clear off and let me get some sleep, else I'll not be responsible for what I do. . . ."

He was an ugly, thick-set, dark little man, with a crooked nose and thick lips. Considerably smaller than his wife, but very strong looking. He had carroty hair, too, and looked like being a tartar if roused.

All the same, Littlejohn was determined to get the answer to the question he'd travelled all night to ask.

"What was in the registered letter your wife sent you the day after the crime, Doakes?"

"I've told you there was no letter. . . ."

And Doakes turned on his heel and walked off.

Littlejohn followed him and took him by the collar. There was nothing else for it.

Doakes turned and lunged at Littlejohn. His fighting blood was suddenly up and he saw red. Littlejohn didn't relax his grip on the collar, but drew the jacket half-way down Doakes's back and pinned his arms with it. The sailor was handy with his feet, though, and kicked the police sergeant soundly in the shin. There was a free-for-all for a few minutes. Some deck-hands watched the scuffle but didn't join in. They knew better.

It ended by Doakes being frog-marched to a taxi and taken to the dock police station, where he was charged with obstructing the police.

He was searched, much against his will. They found the registered packet in the pocket of a body-belt. It contained fifty pounds in notes! There was a letter with it.

> Dear Jack,
> I wish you'd stop pestering me every time you get in port. You know we don't hit it and the sooner we end it the better. What you want a hundred pounds for, I don't know. And as for saying if I don't send it you'll make it hot for me—well—do your worst. I don't care.
> . . . For old times sake, I'm sending you fifty pounds. That's final. Not another penny. . . .

Doakes was discharged with a caution, and went off after telling Littlejohn he'd swing for him if ever their paths crossed again.

Their paths crossed almost at once, but Doakes ignored Littlejohn, who had been interviewing the skipper of the *Maid of Morven*.

"I wish you'd come to me first, instead of kicking up all that fuss. I could have told you everything about Doakes."

The captain was a lanky, rugged Scot, who didn't smoke or drink and read his Bible a lot. He didn't like roughhouses on his ship, though nobody aboard was handier with his fists when justly provoked.

"Doakes is quite a decent chap, according to his lights. Once at sea, no captain could ask for a better officer. In port, he drinks too much, but there's little wrong in him."

"He must spend a lot on drink, sir. He's not only gone through his own pay, but sponges on his wife, with whom, from all accounts, he doesn't get on well."

"He's been unlucky matrimonially, that's true. But, from what he tells me, that's not his fault. His wife has always been off with other men as soon as he's got to sea. Doakes himself is very decent where women are concerned. Never had anything with which to reproach him there. Two years ago, however, he took up with a girl in the dock canteen here, and when we got in port this time he found there was a baby. He did the right thing as far as he could. Set her up in a home of her own just outside the town and gave her money. And he's going to marry her as soon as he can. He's just filed papers for divorce against Mrs. Doakes. He promised me he'd marry the other girl. I'll knock the living daylights out of him if he doesn't. She happens to be my niece. . . ."

Littlejohn got a bath and some breakfast and caught the nine o'clock back to Fetling. He felt very foolish and out of temper with himself, for he had made a fool's errand. And he'd a vague feeling that someone was behind it.

However, he fell asleep and slept most of the journey. When he awoke, he felt better, and made up his mind that somebody was going to sit-up for last night's work. Who, he didn't know. It was like fighting in the dark. . . .

On his way to his hotel he called at *The Seven Whistlers*. The shop was open and Small and Mrs. Doakes were in it, although there were no customers.

"You again!" said Small. But he didn't look very comfortable. He seemed a bit more favourably disposed towards the police, to whom he looked to catch his burglars.

Mrs. Doakes ignored Littlejohn and went on dusting some furniture.

"I hear you've had burglars, Mr. Small? Did they take much?"

"As far as I can see, not a thing. I must have scared 'em away. Got home sooner than usual last night, and they must have been startin'. Whoever it was hid in the boxroom upstairs and when I went in coshed me good and proper with somethin'. I feel like nothin' on earth this morning."

Littlejohn's old good-humour returned. Small had evidently been figuring as an ill-treated hero. In his imagination the old cloth in which Littlejohn had wrapped him had changed to a cosh or knuckle-duster!

And Small had been liberally fortifying himself already. The place reeked of whisky.

"So the thieves didn't get anything?"

"Ransacked the place for valuables. Turned Mrs. Doakes's bedroom upside down, and you never saw such a mess as they left mine in. . . ."

Well, well!

"I suppose the police here have the matter in hand."

"Yes. But they're a slow lot. They'll never get who done it. Two men came down last night—Sergeant and a constable—but they seemed they didn't know which end to start of. Said it was probably some local small-fry. Perhaps it was—I dunno. It's upsettin', though, when you can't leave the place for an hour without it bein' broke into. And a bobby supposed to be on the beat, too."

Mrs. Doakes snorted, but didn't raise her head.

"By the way, Mr. Small. You said you came home early. Why did you do that, last night of all nights?"

"Funny thing, now. I'd been at the Bay Hotel for a bit when someone rang me up. About nine, it'ud be. Didn't say who they was, but just that they'd been passin' my place and thought they saw somebody goin' in by the back door. Thought they'd better let me know. So I come to see."

Mrs. Doakes rose and put her hand on her hips.

"Thought you said you weren't so well and that's what brought you home. . . ."

"Didn't want to alarm you. Didn't seem to be nobody

about. 'ow was I to know they was hidin' in the upstairs rooms?"

"Didn't want to alarm me, indeed . . . !"

Mrs. Doakes resumed her polishing. The pair of them were half-dressed and unwashed again. They looked ready for a good row when the Inspector had left them. So he went.

At the police-station he found Gillespie in a good humour, which clouded over when Littlejohn told of his night's adventures. The Superintendent had looked a bit sheepish as the Inspector entered and caught him stitching a button on his pants.

"Just had a bit of an accident, and the distaff-side, as you might call 'em, being away from home, I'm executing running repairs. . . ."

Littlejohn grinned.

"Want any help?"

"Well, Littlejohn, what do we do next? Looks as though we've struck another dead-end."

"Yes. I think I'll have a meal at my hotel and then rest a bit. I feel all-in after last night's trip."

"What about a bit of lunch together?"

"I'll just get a snack, if you don't mind, and then snooze for a while."

"Right-o! See you later. Sorry about the lost journey."

They found Littlejohn some chicken sandwiches at his hotel. He ate them with a pint of beer. It was a warm, sunny day, and it might not be bad to take a deck-chair on the shore and snatch forty-winks there.

There weren't many people about in the spot he chose, and he sat for some time watching the receding tide. Children were making sand-pies and erecting castles on the damp shore, gulls swooped and cried overhead, and in the distance a destroyer was flashing signals to a shore station. A few boats bobbed about on the water and some late bathers were splashing about in the deeper parts. It was very restful. . . .

It was cold when Littlejohn awoke. The tide was far out and all the holidaymakers had gone in to tea. Even the gulls had cleared off. The blue sky had clouded over and the water was like lead. It gave rise to melancholy thoughts.

Something must have happened to Littlejohn's mind during his snooze. When he came to himself he was obsessed by a fearful thought. He tried to dismiss it, but it persisted. He realised that he would dispel it only by proving it untrue.

He slowly folded up his deck-chair and took it back to the old lady from whom he had hired it. And when he paid her he forgot to wait for his change.

Gillespie was not at the police-station, so Littlejohn asked the sergeant for Robinshaw's holiday address. He had been getting information for Littlejohn, who had forgotten to ask him about something before he left.

Then, the Inspector put through a trunk call and managed to catch Robinshaw, who was just having afternoon tea with his beloved and his mother-in-law-to-be.

## ◂ 18 ▸

### THE TOWING PATH

ROBINSHAW sounded very pleased with himself over the telephone. Littlejohn asked him a few details about his share in the investigation before his departure for holidays, and then casually passed on to small-talk about the weather and how the party were enjoying themselves.

"Fine," answered Robinshaw, and Littlejohn could almost see him rubbing his hands with pleasure. The presence of Mrs. Gillespie didn't seem to bother him at all.

"Mrs. Gillespie all right?"

"Yes. Havin' a good time. Didn't like leaving her husband behind, but he wanted it. Couldn't come himself with a murder on his hands, but didn't mind Mrs. Gillespie coming. In fact, he suggested it at the start and almost insisted. Said she needed a rest. . . ."

Littlejohn felt more depressed than ever after that.

The Superintendent was out at the time, so Littlejohn had a word with the sergeant-in-charge.

"By the way, could you tell me, sergeant, which constables would be on the Laurieston beat when Miss Curwen lived there? Say, for twelve months before she removed."

The sergeant, who resembled an enormous moustached bulldog, grated a large forefinger over his stubbly chin. He was not very active physically, but he had a good memory.

"Mostly Quinland and Robinshaw, sir."

"Robinshaw, eh?"

"Yes. He's not been in plain-clothes long. Got on rather fast. . . ."

There was a peevish note in the sergeant's voice, suggesting that Robinshaw had perhaps been unduly pushed up the ladder of promotion.

"What about Quinland?"

"He was transferred to the Glesdon force about three months since. Glesdon's four miles away inland. A small town with about ten of a force, and under the county, like us."

"I see. How do you get there?"

"Bus is best. Every half hour. Or it's a nice walk along the towing-path of the canal. Through the country. A lot of people walk in that way."

"Thanks, sergeant."

"Anything more I can do, sir?"

"No, thanks."

Littlejohn took the next bus to Glesdon. Quinland was off duty, for it was his week on night patrol. The Inspector found him digging potatoes in his back garden. A youngish, fresh-faced officer, whose wife had gone to the pictures and left him minding the youngsters. Two small boys were sorting out the potatoes as their father unearthed them. All three were sweating, grimy and busy.

Quinland was sheepish about being found in such a dishevelled state by a high-ranker from Scotland Yard. He apologised two or three times, until Littlejohn told him to stop it, then, after setting the two lads to work digging themselves to keep them out of mischief, the constable took Littlejohn to a little summer-house he had built and there they talked and smoked.

"I hear you used often to be on the beat which took you past Laurieston at nights, Quinland."

"Yes, sir."

"You'd know pretty well all that came and went at Laurieston, then?"

"Yes, sir. . . ."

Quinland was beginning to swallow hard and to eye the tip of his cigarette instead of meeting Littlejohn's look.

"Had they many visitors at night?"

"Not many. When the old man was alive, he went early to bed, I know. Miss Curwen's lady friends used to call. I got used to them. I sort of kept a watchful eye on the place. A big house, with plenty of good stuff in it, specially silver. And with there being only a lady and an old man there, it was as well. . . ."

"Any male visitors?"

Quinland cleared his throat and paused.

"Now this is vitally important, Quinland, and concerns the Fetling murder case. You can tell me everything without fear of suffering, if that's what's making you reticent."

Quinland looked hot and bothered.

"Well, the murdered man went there once a week or so. That was while Mr. Curwen was bedridden—three months before he died. And after he died, too, Grossman would call. I was moved soon after."

"Why?"

"I really don't know. It was just one of those moves we all have to expect, I suppose. Came from county headquarters."

"You've perhaps guessed why you were moved. Now, come along, Quinland. I want the truth. Who else used to call on Miss Curwen?"

"I . . . I . . ."

"Was it Superintendent Gillespie?"

"How did you know, sir?"

"Was it?"

168

"Yes, sir."

Quinland looked like a boy caught stealing apples. His heart was in his boots, for he saw all hopes of promotion vanishing into air.

"Did he call often?"

"Perhaps twice a week."

"During Mr. Mark's lifetime?"

"Towards the end of it and after he died till I was moved."

"Why were you moved?"

"Well . . ."

"Did you tell the Superintendent you'd seen him there?"

"Not exactly, sir. I saw him several times without him seeing me. But one night I bumped right into him as he was coming out of the gate. Of course, I bid him goodnight. . . ."

"Perhaps rather tactless of you. Go on."

"Shortly after, the county people wanted somebody here and sent for me. I had to find a house, and here I am."

"Thank you, Quinland. And now, not a word of this to a soul. . . ."

"Not likely, sir. I've had enough of speaking out of my turn. I liked Fetling, and so did the wife. We were sore at this move, especially as it wasn't what you'd call promotion. . . ."

Littlejohn walked back along the towing-path. He felt the need of quiet thought, and this was the most peaceful spot. He lit his pipe and started on his way. Dusk was falling and there was hardly a soul about.

It was Gillespie's laugh at Littlejohn's discomfiture at *The Seven Whistlers* that had started it all. It was not the sort of laugh one gives at a humorous situation, but a mirthless neigh of triumph. At least that is how it seemed to Littlejohn, and he always trusted first impressions.

Then, someone had warned Small that his premises were being entered. Littlejohn traced back in his mind his every step of the previous night. He had been caution itself. It looked as though someone who knew he was going had . . .

If Small had caught him there, Littlejohn would have been quite unable to justify himself. No search warrant, no reasonable excuse. To say the least of it, he'd have been in a tight corner, and most certainly, if Small had pressed it, would have been recalled to London, if not reduced in rank for unauthorised entry.

Who would have benefited by such a betrayal?

Finally, Quinland's shattering revelation. Gillespie had been in the habit of calling at the Curwens unseen! And this went on even after old Mark's death. . . .

The long stretch of placid water had turned dark green under the clear twilight. The arches of the bridges which bore the roads across the canal were reflected in the water, forming complete circles, half real, half pictures.

Fishermen were packing-up their stools and tackle and going home.

A motor-barge with two butties trailing behind slowly passed. The man steering withdrew his pipe, spat in the canal, and bade Littlejohn good evening. He looked so contented. Not a care in the world. His wife was dying in a hospital not far away and his only boy had been killed in the war. You never knew. . . . Despair brings its own form of resignation.

The tarred and whitewashed cottages on the banks were beginning to light up. The reflections from their windows shone in the water. A belated crowd of ducks, dignified and orderly, swam eagerly to their shed on the far side and entered, quacking delightedly.

So Gillespie was deep in the case, not as a policeman, but

as a party on the other side. And he had said nothing. He had got rid of his wife and family, too, and was alone in the house.

If the Superintendent had all that on his mind, no wonder he was moody and bilious. Not his liver, but his conscience, must be troubling him.

The towing-path led right into the town of Fetling. It was dark when Littlejohn got there. He was very depressed and wished he'd never seen the place.

The case against Mrs. Doakes had not exactly collapsed like a pack of cards, but had now become a remote possibility. True, the diamonds might have been sent in the registered package to John Doakes, but he and his wife were on poor terms and he was dunning her for money. She would hardly, in such circumstances, trust him with thousands of pounds' worth of jewellery. Had she disposed of it elsewhere? Or had she had it at all?

Nobody saw Mrs. Doakes on the train on which Grossman was killed. And her alibi was weak, but not impossible. She might have been in the pictures all the time the murder was going on.

It meant starting all over again and sifting every bit of information carefully. This time Littlejohn was alone. Gillespie couldn't be regarded as a collaborator any more, and with him his police force went out of commission, too.

Littlejohn rang up Miss Teare, the friend of Barbara Curwen. He wanted to know where he could find Lucy, the maid. Luckily, Miss Teare was in and told him that Lucy had finished at Barbara's flat and gone home. She lived in Fetling. Miss Teare gave Littlejohn her address.

Lucy's mother kept a third-rate boarding house in a back street. A small, fat, half-washed-looking woman, she opened the door for Littlejohn and eyed him up and down under the hall lamp. She thought he was after rooms and summed him up as above the average, and therefore was ready to screw up her prices a bit.

"Wantin' a room?"

"No, thank you. Is Lucy in?"

"Yes. Why? What's she bin up to again?"

"Nothing. I'm a police-officer and want to see her concerning the death of Miss Curwen."

"You're only just in time; she's upstairs dollin' herself up ready for the pictures. The sooner she gets work the better. That'll keep her out of mischief. Gaddin' about . . ."

Lucy must have been listening over the balusters, for her head suddenly appeared round them.

"What is it, ma?"

"A policeman wants you. Come down, and be quick."

"I'll just put me frock on. Won't be a jiffy. . . ."

The "jiffy" lasted about a quarter of an hour. Lucy was evidently preparing a full toilet for the benefit of Littlejohn or somebody else who was later going to escort her to the films.

Meanwhile, Littlejohn had to put up with the chatter of her mother in a front room stuffy from lack of open windows and cluttered up with cheap furniture. Now and then boarders entered, went upstairs almost furtively, as though expecting the landlady to rush out and challenge them, and could be heard slamming doors, running water and talking in undertones. Next door, somebody was playing a piano. The strings vibrated like tin and a woman started to sing a popular song in a shrill, affected voice.

Lucy arrived, got-up to kill. Out of her uniform and dressed in a costume and rakish little hat, she didn't seem the same person. She had overdone her make-up and looked like a street-walker.

"Well!!" said her mother. "You do look a fright! Go up

and take some of that paint off this minute. I'm a respectable woman and this is a respectable house. . . ."

"I won't be ordered about and called in front of strangers. . . ."

The two women were squaring-up ready for a good set-to. Littlejohn got cross.

"Stop it! I've waited here long enough. I want a word or two with you, Lucy. You can settle your differences after I've gone."

"What the gentleman thinks of you, I don't know. But I know what I think. . . ."

"I want a word with Lucy alone, please, Mrs. Lewney."

There was a card stuck in the frame of a glass overmantel.

MRS. LEWNEY,
*Select Apartments.*

So the girl was called Lucy Lewney! Good heavens, what a name!

Mrs. Lewney didn't like being shut out, and took it in bad grace. She could be heard out in the lobby giving a boarder the length of her tongue for bringing a woman in with him.

"This is a respectable house. . . ."

Select apartments!

"Now, Lucy, I want you to cast your mind back to the time when you were with Miss Curwen and tell me what you remember about things I ask you."

Lucy sat down in a creaking basket-chair and tried to look attentive and good. She put her ankles together and pulled her frock down over her knees. That was the way they did these things on the pictures. The innocent girl dragged into a sordid scandal . . .

"How long were you with the Curwens?"

"Five years. Started when I left school."

"You remember Mr. Grossman calling?"

"Yes. He came quite a lot."

"Have you any idea what started those visits?"

"It was no business of mine, but I got a good idea. I don't miss much. . . ."

"I'm sure you don't."

Out in the passage the bickering had developed into a full-blown brawl.

"Take your bag and baggage and get out. This is a respectable 'ome. I won't 'ave no carryings-on here. . . ."

Lucy flapped her hands at Littlejohn, indicating that such a vulgar display was abhorrent to her.

"Mr. Grossman started calling when Mr. Mark began to sell his collections. He'd been keen on glass, china and furniture, had Mr. Mark. But he got feeble when he was old and hadn't got the interest in them he had. I heard Miss Barbara tell 'im once that markets were at the top because the Americans were after things, and that he'd better sell if he wanted good prices. So they got Mr. Grossman to come."

"He came a lot after that, didn't he?"

Lucy sniggered.

"Got sweet on Miss Barbara. Rum goings-on. . . ."

"Were there other callers? Men, I mean."

Lucy smiled like Mona Lisa. But said nothing.

"Come along now, Lucy. You don't want to have to tell these things in court, do you? Better tell me quietly here."

Quietly! The battle in the hall had developed. They sounded to be launching an attack on the stairs. In a room above somebody was slamming doors and banging drawers, and shrill voices provided an accompaniment.

"Well, the police called a time or two."

"What for?"

"There was an attempted robbery. Somebody tried to get in through the kitchen window but must have got scared off. Nothing would do for Mr. Mark but send for the police."

"Who came up?"

"A sergeant, and then the Super himself."

**"Mr. Gillespie?"**

"Yes."

Lucy smiled another Mona Lisa.

"How many times did he call?"

"I lost count. He became a regular visitor after that."

"Did he call to see Mr. Mark?"

Lucy laughed outright.

"Not he. He fell for Miss Barbara, too, though I shouldn't be talking like that about the police."

"And he came after Mr. Mark's death?"

"Yes. Right to Mr. Grossman's death. Then he stopped."

"I see. When did he call?"

"Mostly evenings, after I'd gone. I was day-maid and slept here. But I heard and saw him a time or two. I knew all that went on at Laurieston. . . ."

"I'll bet you did."

"Yes. And it's a funny thing, Mr. Gillespie nearly bought that box that Mr. Grossman was found in. Thinkin' things over after you talked to me, I suddenly remembered it. His wife was wantin' one and as Mr. Mark was selling stuff, Mr. Gillespie came to buy it. I overheard him and Miss Barbara talking one day about it."

"And why didn't he take it?"

"Too big, or something. Gave back-word at the last minute. His wife wanted a smaller one. He even took the key of the box. . . ."

"The key! What do you mean? That went to *The Seven Whistlers.*"

"No. The second key, I mean. The one Miss Barbara had."

"But you told me yourself there wasn't another key. Why did you do that?"

"I . . . I . . ."

"Were you told to say nothing about Mr. Gillespie's calling there?"

"Yes."

"By whom?"

"Miss Barbara. Said she'd sack me at a moment's notice and give me no references if I said a word. I daren't risk that. My ma thought the world of Miss Barbara and would have had the hide off me if I'd had the sack. . . ."

I'll say she would, thought Littlejohn. Mrs. Lewney had now reached the state of conflict where one throws the bags down the stairs. The lodger could be heard descending after them, swearing like a trooper, with Mrs. Lewney after him, giving as much as she was getting.

"And don't you dare show your face here again. Respectable house, this is. . . ."

"How did Mr. Gillespie get the other key?"

"I saw Miss Barbara give it to him. 'You might as well take this,' she says, and he puts it in his waistcoat pocket. And the look he gave her. Proper sweet on each other they was. . . ."

"And was Mr. Grossman in the running at the same time?"

"Yes. Though I don't know . . ."

"Never mind that. Now, not a word to anyone about this, Lucy. Not even to your mother."

"As if I would. I know better than talkin' scandal about the police. Once they get their knife in you, you're done for."

"I'm glad you've such a healthy idea of us, Lucy."

Lucy Lewney smiled coyly.

"'ave you two not done yet? I want this room. . . ."

Mrs. Lewney, snorting and palpitating from her moral exertions, glared and started to dust furiously about.

"Yes. I'll be going now. Thank you both."

"You 'eard that. Glad you did. The police'll know now that this is a respectable 'ouse. Takin' a woman up to 'is bedroom, he was. Said they'd an hour to wait for the pictures and he couldn't have 'er standin' about in the cold. I'll give 'im cold. This is a respectable . . ."

It looked as though Mrs. Lewney had been putting on a special show for the benefit of the police!

## 19

### A FRESH START

IT meant starting all over again, and this time it was a grim, solitary battle for Littlejohn.

It was bad enough pursuing a layman for murder. But now a police officer was involved. Gillespie was in it up to the neck!

It was extremely difficult making investigations concerning the movements of a colleague in the police, but it had to be done.

The railway station was almost deserted when the Inspector called there. That dismal, depressing atmosphere of between-trains which surrounds a terminus at night. The stationmaster's office was closed and all his staff had gone home. A foreman porter was in charge of the place. The night shift were working in the parcels office.

Littlejohn drifted casually in among the baggage and large, brown-paper packages.

"Two—Willesden Junction; Four—Leicester; One—East Croydon; Six—Manchester . . ."

They were still hard at it.

A new clerk was in charge. He was dressed in flannel trousers and a sports jacket and looked doped already with the monotonous repetition of the work.

"Let me see, were you on duty the night the man was murdered in the train from here?"

The clerk looked up from his book and stuck his pencil behind his ear.

"Yes. Why?"

"I'm on the case."

"Oh, I see. Not gettin' on so fast, eh?"

"Can't say we are. It's a very difficult nut to crack. By the way, was my colleague Gillespie here on the day it happened?"

"Yes. There'd been some thieving. Several packages of cigarettes opened. In fact, it got so bad we had to call in the police. Two hands were caught and fined. Ought to have gone to gaol by rights, but it was a first offence."

"Three—Bletchley; Seven—Clapham Junction; One—Sevenoaks . . ."

A cold wind blew through the station, scattering bits of paper and throwing up the dust.

"Oh. The Superintendent himself was on the job! What time?"

"About half an hour before Grossman's train went out. I remember remarking about it. The police nearly always get there too late; this time they were too soon. Uh, uh, uh . . ."

The man was offensive, but Littlejohn let him be.

It was dangerous to pursue the matter further. The buffet was still open, so Littlejohn went and bought himself a cup of tea. It was poor stuff but it warmed him up. The foreman porter passed and the girl at the counter called him and handed him a free drink. She rolled her eyes at him as she did so. He was evidently a favourite.

"Cold night," said Littlejohn.

"Yes. Be glad when the last train's gone and I can get to the fire. I'm chilled to the marrer. . . ."

He winked at the girl and raised his cup in a sort of mock toast.

"All the best, Bessie."

"I hear the police were here just before the murder of Grossman the other day. Pity they didn't stay."

"Yes. I've made the same remark myself. You're on the case, aren't you? Looks like being one of the unsolved mysteries, if you ask me. Perfect crime, eh? Nobody seen who did it; whoever did it left no trace, eh?"

He sniffed, wiped his mouth on the back of his hand, and looked delighted with his own wisdom.

"It's a teaser and no mistake. Were you on duty when the London train went out with Mr. Grossman aboard?"

"Yes. I was on the platform. Never saw nobody suspicious about. It beats me how the murderer got on and off the train."

"I suppose you saw Superintendent Gillespie on the station just before it left?"

"Not just then. No. He'd been here about the pinchin' of some cigarettes. Left about half an hour before. I saw him goin' off in the direction of the town then. Pity he didn't stay to hold the little chap's hand, eh?"

Littlejohn went disconsolately away and started to climb the steps of the narrow, sloping street past *The Seven Whistlers*. The shop was closed but there was a light shining through the open door of the back premises. The inspector determined once and for all to put Mrs. Doakes out of the running if he could. He rattled the door handle until she appeared. She was doing the books, it seemed, before she set out for the evening. She wasn't pleased to see him.

"You here again! Pity you can't keep proper hours. The shop's closed and I'm busy."

"I won't keep you a minute. May I come in?"

Mrs. Doakes led the way through the shop to the room behind. It was as untidy as ever and the sink was full of dirty dishes.

"Glad you're not stopping for long. I'm going out."

"I wanted to talk to you about your alibi on the night Mr. Grossman was murdered. It wasn't a very good one, you know."

"What do you mean? I said I was in the pictures, didn't I? And I meant it. I was seen going in and coming out. What more do you want?"

"It's easy to get out once you're in, and in once you're out without being seen, you know. I mean, if you'd wanted to get out meanwhile you could well have done so."

"Well, I didn't. Why should I? You're not thinking *I* murdered Grossman, are you? You are!! I do believe you are!! Well, I like that! What should I want to murder Grossman for? He was more use to me alive than dead."

"What do you mean?"

"Who do you think made all the profits of this place? Not Small. He's drunk half his time and makes as many losses when he's boozed as gains when he's sober. No. Grossman made the money here. Bought cheap in the provinces and sold dear in London. And knew what he was selling. I get a cut of the profits. I wouldn't be likely to kill the goose that lays the golden eggs."

"Not if he had a pocketful of diamonds to make it worth while?"

"What are you getting at?"

"The Coatcliffe necklace. Grossman bought that from Jameson. Wasn't he taking it to hawk in London when he was murdered? And weren't you and Small aware of it?"

Mrs. Doakes's eyes bulged, she caught her breath, and then roared with laughter.

"So that's what you've been getting at. Well, that's a good one! That damned necklace wasn't here when Grossman got his packet. It was sold and far enough away from Fetling."

"How do you know that?"

"I may as well tell you. Grossman's dead and past harming. You seem to know he was a fence. So did Small and me, although he never said a word about it. And I twigged how he got rid of the stuff, too. There's a Dutch boat puts in here from time to time. The skipper's a Captain Cornelius. He always called to see Grossman when he docked. Anybody more unlike Grossman's type you couldn't imagine. Yet they'd spend the evening together at Grossy's flat regularly. That's where the stuff went. Direct from here to the Continent. Cornelius called just after the Jameson Raid, as me and Small called it for fun, and was sure to take the diamonds off with him. If you want a motive for me killing Grossman, don't try that. I wanted him alive; not dead."

The woman spoke with quiet conviction, and Littlejohn believed her. In fact, he was ready from the start to cross her off as a suspect. All he wanted was some assurance.

"So you suspect me? Well, I'll have to better my alibi, then, though I didn't want to mention this. If you'll not make it public, I'll tell you. I was in the pictures with somebody who can prove I was there. I met him inside and was with him all the time."

"Why?"

"He's divorced his wife and the decree absolute isn't through yet. Doakes and me are getting a divorce, too, and then my friend's marrying me, see? We want no slip-up, so I see him on the quiet at present."

"Oh. Well, if I want his name I'll ask you for it then. I'm glad you told me this. I'll probably manage without his confirmation, but I shall expect the name if I need it."

"O.K. Decent of you. That's why I've been a bit awkward about this affair. It means a lot to me, marrying and settling down with my friend."

"Right. I won't keep you longer, Mrs. Doakes. Good night."

"Good night, Inspector."

Littlejohn had no inclination to return to the police station. He felt no desire to face Gillespie without having made up his mind what to do about the Superintendent's part in the affair. He must think about it first.

The promenade lights were on and the tide was in. Most of the people were indoors at one or another of the amusements and only a few strollers were taking the air. A chill wind was blowing. Littlejohn lit his pipe and sat in one of the shelters facing the sea. In the distance you could see the intermittent rays of a lighthouse and in the foreground the riding lights of two boats making for the old harbour.

First of all, suppose that Gillespie had been involved in a love affair with Barbara Curwen. He didn't look the romantic sort, but it might happen to anyone.

Grossman was also connected in some way with Barbara. London reports said he'd stayed with her at the same hotel. Was she running the pair of them?

If so, it might easily be a case of jealousy, or blackmail, or both. Gillespie might have discovered Grossman's part in the matter and killed him.

Or, more likely, a little crook like Grossman might have got hold of something against Gillespie and the Superintendent might have murdered him to quieten him.

All very well, but again a theory. It might all fizzle out just as in the case of Mrs. Doakes.

The shelter in which Littlejohn was sitting had a separate landward side, and behind the partition two lovers were quarrelling. The sound of them provided a relief from the Inspector's own unhappy thoughts.

"You know he doesn't mean anything to me. . . ."

"The way you look at him when you're dancing's enough. . . ."

"Are you trying to pick a quarrel . . . ?"

"No, but I'm fed up with the way you go on. . . ."

The eternal squabble. Old as Adam and Eve.

Some hooligans larking along the promenade threw a fire-cracker at a passing couple and a violent row arose between the riff-raff and the offended parties.

But Gillespie had the second key. That was it! If only there was some way of bringing it home to Gillespie. . . .

It would have been easy for him to kill Grossman. Especially if Barbara Curwen knew and told Gillespie that Grossman was going on a certain train. But she was in London. Had she telephoned Gillespie? The box was large enough for Gillespie's body. After all, he wasn't as big as Littlejohn, and the Inspector felt he could have squeezed himself into the chest at a pinch for a very limited period.

He remembered Gillespie sewing on a button with needle and cotton. Perhaps he'd used his skill on the packing round the box, as well.

So, there it was, the new theory.

Gillespie decides to kill Grossman for some reason or other. Blackmail or jealousy. He learns, probably from Barbara, that Grossman's travelling on a certain train to London. He seeks a way of getting at the little man unseen by anyone.

Through the sidings, as previously it had been assumed Mrs. Doakes had done. And he has learned, almost fortuitously, that the chest is going by the same train.

He boards the train unseen, and whilst the guard is prowling for tickets, hides in the box, the packing of which he's loosened. Then, the coast clear, Grossman's body, unconscious, replaces that of Gillespie. The box is locked, the packing sewn up, and Gillespie sneaks out at the next stop and returns to Fetling.

The lovers were still hard at it.

"If you loved me, you wouldn't suspect me of things like that. . . ."

"If you loved me, you wouldn't do them. . . ."

"Oh, very well, if you're tired of me . . ."

Littlejohn could almost have told them what to say next. The funny thing was that Littlejohn had told it all to Gillespie in reference to Mrs. Doakes. No wonder Gillespie laughed! In his position of confidence he could see the net tightening around the wrong person and was glad to let it do so. He even helped it along. Telephoned Small and launched him on Littlejohn right in the middle of his job of amateur burglary!

And he'd almost got away with it! If Doakes and his wife had not been on bad terms, and if Quinland hadn't happened to stumble across the Superintendent during his visits to Laurieston . . .

Gillespie might have killed Barbara Curwen, too. Or, maybe it was suicide. Perhaps she hadn't been able to bear the idea of one man killing another through her.

Or, again, after being questioned about the second key and lying by saying she'd given it Grossman instead of Gillespie, she may have tackled Gillespie about his share in the crime and he, finding her a menace, had killed her.

That crime might never be solved. It had the characteristics of a suicide. . . .

The lovers on the other side of the shelter were making it up.

"I didn't mean what I said. You know it's you I love . . ."

"If I lost you, I'd kill myself. . . ."

Littlejohn had had enough about killing for one night. He made off to a telephone kiosk to ring up Scotland Yard and have them immediately check any calls Barbara Curwen might have made from her hotel. It was a long shot but might bring in results. They were to ring his hotel and tell him at whatever hour the information came.

The now happy pair were kissing in the shelter.

I wish everything ended happy ever after, thought Littlejohn. And with his head down and his shoulders hunched, he sorrowfully made for his hotel.

## 20

### THE QUIET HOUSE

SCOTLAND YARD came on at half-past two in the morning.

Luckily, there was an instrument in every bedroom at Littlejohn's hotel, so he hadn't to get up and go down for the call. But the night-porter was annoyed. He'd been having a snooze. Some of the guests had no consideration at all. . . .

Barbara Curwen had rung-up Fetling 2222 on the day Grossman died. That was the number of Fetling police station!

That settled it. Littlejohn slept no more that night. He tossed and turned and, in the end, in desperation, made an enemy for life of the night-porter by ringing up his home at Hampstead at four in the morning. There was a bedside telephone between their two beds there.

"My God, I'm glad to hear your voice, Letty."

"Whatever's the matter. Are you ill?"

"No. Worse. It's this case. It's got me down."

"I've never heard you say that before. Whatever is it? Are you in danger?"

"No. I think I've solved it, and it's appalling."

"Can't you tell me?"

"Remember the Crossbank case . . . It's the same sort of criminal."

"Oh. . . ."

She understood!

"Like me to come down and collect you in the car when it's over?"

"I'd be glad if you would. Sorry I can't ask you to stay a day or two. The sooner I get away from this damned place the better. . . ."

"Wherever have you been? I thought they'd be fishing *you* out of the sea next," said Gillespie when Littlejohn entered his room early next morning.

"No. Some new developments kept me busy and you were out when I called early in the evening."

"Just shopping. On my own, you know. Anything to report?"

Gillespie spoke slowly, staring straight at Littlejohn as though he'd sensed a change in the Inspector's manner. His hands alone betrayed his nervous tension. They were gripped tightly, one in the other, across the desk.

"What did you do with the second key when Miss Curwen gave it to you some time ago, Superintendent?"

The hands relaxed and stayed limp. Gillespie's face grew strangely composed. You wouldn't have thought it possible in the teeth of such a startling question.

"Here," he said, and taking it from his pocket, rose, placed it on the corner of his desk nearest Littlejohn with his left hand and delivered a crashing blow on the point of the Inspector's chin with his right.

Then he rang for the sergeant.

"Inspector Littlejohn's just gone over, Smith," he said when the man entered with heavy feet. "He's been up on the case all night and seems all in. Help me with him to my car and I'll see him to his hotel and get a doctor. The man's been at it too hard."

"But—but . . . Oughtn't we to bring him round first, sir? It'll be easier then."

"Do as you're told, Smith. Bed and a doctor's what's wanted right away."

They took Littlejohn under the armpits and settled him in the car.

"Like me to come with you, sir?"

"No. I'll manage him, Smith. You see to things here."

Instead of the hotel, Gillespie took Littlejohn to his own home. And he tied him up properly with Mrs. Gillespie's clothes-line.

When Littlejohn came to himself he was seated in a chair near the dining table and Gillespie was pouring brandy down his throat from a tumbler.

"Sorry to do this, Littlejohn, but it had to be. Drink. You'll feel better after it. Don't struggle with the ropes, you'll only hurt yourself. You can't get free. I'm good at knots. . . ."

There was a revolver on the table beside the brandy bottle.

Gillespie was pale but very collected. By his manner the pair of them might still have been collaborating on the case.

"I want a long talk with you and I'm sorry I've had to truss you up . . . I know you'll not shout. You're not that sort. But if you do, I shall stick a dirty duster in your mouth, so you'd best not."

There was almost an air of benevolent jocularity about the man. He was either greatly relieved or going demented.

"When I got in last night, the sergeant told me you'd been enquiring about Robinshaw and Quinland. I knew then the game was up. I spent all night deciding what to do. The decision's very simple. But first, I want a long talk with you. Don't worry; this isn't going to be like a bit of sensational fiction. I want to exchange information, Littlejohn, as professional to professional, and then I'll tell you what I propose to do. . . ."

"I suppose I ought to tell you, Gillespie, that you won't get away with it. However, carry on. Get it over quickly. I haven't slept all night, either, and that knock-out provided the finishing touches to a very unpleasant headache."

"I'm sorry."

The house was as quiet as the grave, except for the purring of an electric clock over the fireplace.

Outside in the road, people were going about their morning business. A woman pushing a perambulator and holding another child by the hand. An elderly man in a battered felt hat carrying a string-bag full of what looked like brussels sprouts. A telegraph boy on a bicycle.

"What started you on this new tack, Littlejohn?"

"I seemed to be chasing my tail all the time, when suddenly the laugh you gave when I was almost caught in Small's place stopped me. And the fact that nobody but the police knew I was going there."

"Yes. I must own up, I slipped there. I almost slipped up, too, in the case of the flag. You remember the Children's Home flag that was found with the body? That was mine. I'd forgotten all about the thing till you suddenly turned up with it. You made me sweat for a bit until it fizzled out."

"Suppose we'd arrested Mrs. Doakes?"

"We couldn't have done. Not enough evidence."

"I agree."

"I knew you'd never find the jewellery. As soon as the robbery occurred I began to watch Grossman. I'd had an eye on him for some time. I knew of the visits of Captain Cornelius and thought they were for no good. That's what started the whole trouble . . . those jewels."

A taxi had drawn up at the house next door. The driver jumped out and rang the bell, and the next thing, he and the owner came staggering down the path with a large trunk which they fastened on the luggage carrier.

A man in a peaked cap on a carrier-bicycle passed, ringing his bell. A woman with a child bought two packets of ice-cream from him, and she and the youngster started greedily to gobble it up.

"Yes; it was the jewels started it all. I knew Birdie Jameson had been seeing Grossman about them . . ."

"From Miss Curwen?"

"Ah, you know that! Yes, she told me. So I tackled Grossman. He produced a packet of letters I'd written to Miss Curwen. I was to pay for part of them and the rest would be security for Grossman's activities as a fence. . . ."

"I thought it might be something like that."

"Yes. I can tell you everything and then you'll see how far your own deductions were right. We shan't be together much longer, you and I, so you might as well have the whole tale."

"You were Barbara Curwen's lover?"

"Don't look so surprised. We met in connection with an attempted robbery at Laurieston. We seemed to take to each other and almost before we knew what was happening, we were in love. . . ."

It was a different Gillespie now speaking. In spite of the situation, he had acquired a new dignity, somehow assuming his manhood again after the domination of a masterful wife.

"I've not much to say in excuse for what I've done. Barbara gave me the only happiness I've had in untold years. And now she's dead. And I don't care what happens to me. . . ."

Almost subconsciously, Littlejohn wondered how this affair was going to finish. Was Gillespie going to try to make a break for it? Or . . . A funny thing, Littlejohn always began to think of his insurance and how Letty would go on if he suddenly met the end. Somehow, Gillespie didn't look like trying to avoid what was due to him. He was too resigned.

Two women next door were going down the path to join the taxi. They were loaded with raincoats, umbrellas, carrier bags and large handbags. They scrambled into the car, which drove off.

"It's all so simple, really. I know I've a reputation for being moody and disagreeable. It's arisen out of sheer unhappiness. When I joined the force I made up my mind to get right to the top of the tree. I worked damned hard. At thirty I was well on the way—an Inspector. Then I got married. Here I am—buried in Fetling. . . ."

Littlejohn didn't know what to say. This was probably the first time Gillespie had opened his heart to anyone. And the last. He didn't look the sort for confidences. He seemed all dry and tight inside.

"I'm not saying anything about Mrs. Gillespie. We're all as nature made us. We can't help or change ourselves. It's been my fault, too. I've asked for too much. Like drawing a cheque when you've not got money in the bank. It comes back with a smack in the eye. . . ."

"Oh, come, come, Gillespie. Life's not as bad as that!"

Littlejohn forgot that he was talking to a self-confessed murderer. Gillespie's intensity carried him away.

"But suppose you get on with the account of the crime."

"You don't want my woes, I know. Barbara Curwen and I were in love. She used to confide everything in me. It was pleasant to have somebody I could talk to as well. I'm not a very confiding sort by nature. She told me about Grossman having met Birdie Jameson at his flat. She was there at the time. She told me he'd been advising her about the sale of the old man's antiques. She also telephoned me from London on the day I killed him, to say that she'd learned he was going down by the 7.45 train. Said he'd wired her. They were to meet and discuss the sale of some of her things at a London auction."

"I see."

"I can tell by the sound of your voice that you think I've been a mug. I have. A real mug. I didn't know, until Scotland Yard found out, that Barbara Curwen had been carrying on with Grossman, too. She swore it ended before I came along. I saw her just before she died. I told her I'd finished with her. I knew she suspected that I'd done for Grossman. I told her outright I had done it, and that she was the cause of it. Yes, it was suicide all right. She must have gone straight from me to Blight Head. When I saw her dead I realised that what she'd said about Grossman and her was true and that she'd loved me. I knew, too, that I'd never love anyone but her and that it wasn't worth going on without her. So here we are. . . ."

Two property repairers slowly ambled past, pushing a hand-cart full of ladders and scaffold-boards. One of them shouted a saucy remark to a passing girl, who tossed her head but looked pleased at whatever was said.

"Your turn now, Littlejohn. Tell me how I did it. . . ."

"Roughly, I'd say that your position was intolerable. You couldn't have Grossman with a hold over you, carrying on activities as a fence, extracting money and all the implications of blackmail. How did he get the letters?"

"Must have rifled a drawer or something at Laurieston. Barbara was surprised when I told her. But it was true. The letters had gone. They told the truth about my feelings and happiness. It wouldn't have done for them to be made public. I've hardly a bean to call my own. Just enough life insurance, that's all. This place is bought on mortgage. My wife has money of her own, but at the rate we live I just make ends meet. I'd got to eliminate Grossman, you see. Well . . . go on."

"You know my views for the most part. I've already told you how I thought Mrs. Doakes boarded the train unseen, laid Grossman out, put him in the box to suffocate, and got out at the next stop and came back to Fetling. The same applies to you, I guess."

"That's it. I hatched it all out in a matter of minutes. I saw the box which they said was going on the same train as Grossman. Barbara had told me the train he was travelling by. I went through the goods yard, crept along the line on the side farthest from the platform, quickly undid the packing and got in the box. It was a large chest, but a tight squeeze."

"I'll say it was."

"The guard went out and I emerged from the box. The corridor was dark and I was lucky in finding Grossman quickly. If I'd been spotted, I'd have said I was going to the next station, and I'd have had to wait till another time. I wasn't seen. . . ."

In the garden opposite, a man in flannels and a sweater was clipping the privet hedge and a woman at the door was telling him how to do it. He went steadily on with the job without heeding a word.

"Grossman nearly had a fit when he saw me. I asked him where the letters were. He said I didn't think him such a fool as to carry them with him. He had a smile on his face I wanted to knock off. I'd put a truncheon in my pocket and I let him have it almost before I realised what I was doing. Then, it dawned on me . . . If Grossman were dead we, the police, would search his flat. I'd find the letters. I did later."

"So you . . ."

"He was unconscious and breathing heavily. I just couldn't kill him with my hands, in cold blood. I took him under the arms and dragged him to the van. If I'd been spotted I'd have said he'd been taken ill. I put him in the box and locked it."

"With the key Miss Curwen had given you long ago."

"Yes. How did you find that out, by the way? The last nail in my coffin, wasn't it?"

"Lucy, the maid, overheard you when Miss Curwen gave it you."

"You know, Littlejohn, I admire your thoroughness. To think of you getting on that. What a damned pity this is ending as it is for you. You know, if it hadn't been for Lord Trotwoode flaring up at the Chief Constable because the dinner at *The Saracen's Head* was foul, I don't think Scotland Yard would have been approached. We'd have handled this ourselves. It would have died a natural death, unsolved. Barbara would still have been alive, and I—I—I'd have been free with her. It's funny how little things—pudding-cloth in this case, according to the tale—how the little things upset life."

"Much oftener than the big ones."

"Yes. Well, I put Grossman in the box, locked him in and stitched up the wrapping . . ."

"With the help of that little bachelor-companion I saw you using to stitch on a button on the night you 'phoned Small about my entering his place?"

"You don't miss much. Yes. I always carried it about. My wife seems too busy to bother with my buttons. And I'm sorry about that 'phone call. Shows how desperate I was. I wanted you out of the way and that was all I could think of."

"If it had come off, I'd have been in a pretty fix."

"I'm glad it didn't now."

In the hall the telephone bell began to ring. *Prr-prr. Prr-prr. Prr-prr.* They sat in silence until it stopped. Gillespie made no move.

"Wonder what that is?"

The house seemed a world apart. Through the window life went on and you didn't seem a part of it at all. Like being on another planet and watching through a powerful telescope strange beings behaving in their own little ways. A window cleaner slowly reared his ladder against the house next door and set about the windows with a washleather. Littlejohn's faculties seemed intensified and small things struck him. The window cleaner wasn't reaching the corners of the panes at all. Just skimping the job.

"I let you go on working away on the Mrs. Doakes angle. If you'd got her hanged I wouldn't have cared. A useless, loose sort of woman, all out for her own ends and good for nobody. Better out of the way. But I'd underestimated you. When I heard that you were after Robinshaw and Quinland, the red light shone. I knew then it wouldn't be long. I worked with you intimately enough to know when once you've got your teeth into a thing you worry it like a terrier. I saw my time was limited and you were approaching relentlessly."

"And now, Gillespie, what about untying me? I'm not scared for my own skin, but you might as well save yourself a lot of trouble. You can't get away, you know. If you kill me, the rest will get you. You see, there's someone knows who did it besides me. . . ."

"I know. I had a talk with the night-porter of *The Saracen's Head* earlier on. You spoke to your wife in the night. He listened-in on the switchboard to kill time waiting for you to finish. He didn't know what it was all about, but I guessed. You told your wife."

"Well? I guess that call, Gillespie, was from the police station trying to find you. She should be here by now and has probably learned that you and I are out together and that you carried me to your car. . . ."

"You think of everything, don't you? Well, they should be along any minute. So . . . I'd better do what's got to be done quick and clean. First, there's a full confession in my drawer at the station. The key's in my pocket. There's a key to this house on the mantelpiece of my room. Just excuse me."

Gillespie went in the hall and could be heard twisting the dial of the 'phone.

"You, Smith? She has, has she? Oh. . . . Very well. I'm at my house and I want you to come here right away. Let yourself in. There's a key to the house on the mantelpiece of my office. Got it? Right. Good-bye, old chap."

At the other end, Smith passed a huge paw over his face and went to find the key and follow instructions.

"Old chap!" Things were looking up!

"Your wife's just gone hunting for you at the hotel where they think I might have taken you. But she'll be here soon, I guess. . . ."

Littlejohn wondered what the next move would be. The window cleaner had finished already and was carrying away his ladder. He peered curiously into the room where the two police officers were sitting, but apparently couldn't make out what was going on. Then he reared his ladder against the Gillespie house and climbed slowly to the upper windows. They could hear his leather squealing on the panes.

"I'm sorry I've held you in suspense, Littlejohn. I should have told you my way out. But I couldn't resist the last bit of drama. Holding the curtain to the end. Although you wouldn't think it, I used to be a good amateur actor once . . . once . . ."

"Well, that's all. The confession. The key. And not much time. I don't suppose you'll want to shake hands with a murderer. In any case, you're too well tied up. I wish we'd been on a more savoury case together; I've grown quite fond of you. . . ."

Gillespie crossed the room, and taking Littlejohn by the shoulder, gave it an affectionate squeeze.

"They'll soon be here, and then you'll be all right. Good-bye."

And with that Gillespie took up the revolver from the table, put the muzzle to his temple, and fired. It all seemed like one sweeping movement.

He stood there for a moment, tottering. Then Littlejohn watched the light die from his eyes, and the body sagged to the ground.